"Come to bed."

In Sandra's bedroom, they undressed each other, kissing. Fear flared again and Sandra caught her breath, holding Jay's face with both hands.

Jay rested her palms on Sandra's hips. "Have you ever made love with a woman?"

Surprised by the question, Sandra said, "Yes, of course. Do I seem so naive?"

"Scared." Jay smiled.

Sandra closed her eyes. Sex didn't scare her, just the risk of self-exposure. She had the feeling that she was venturing onto the narrowest of ledges.

"Underneath the surface," Jay whispered, "love is very soft, very simple."

## About the Author

Lisa Shapiro shares a home in New Hampshire with Lynne D'Orsay, her cherished and honest lover of ten years.

# The Color of Winter

## BY LISA SHAPIRO

THE NAIAD PRESS, INC.
1996

Printed in the United States of America on acid-free paper
First Edition

Editor: Christine Cassidy
Cover designer: Bonnie Liss (Phoenix Graphics)
Typesetter: Sandi Stancil


**Library of Congress Cataloging-in-Publication Data**

Shapiro, Lisa 1962 –
    The color of winter / by Lisa Shapiro.
        p.        cm.
    ISBN 1-56280-116-3 (pbk.)
    1. Teacher-student relationships—Fiction.    2. Lesbians—
Fiction.    I. Title.
PS3569.H34146C65        1996
813'.54—dc20                                                        95-39253
                                                                            CIP

*For Lynne*

# Chapter 1

Autumn arrived in California without fanfare. Foliage failed to riot against fading daylight; still, the days shortened and a chill slipped into evening. Dr. Sandra Ross eyed the West Coast beauty — rusty, fire-weary foothills to the east, the San Francisco skyline thrusting its financial towers into view across the bay. She wasn't used to it. Her footsteps echoed purposefully past stubborn trees whose leaves refused to cooperate with the season.

The University of California at Berkeley campus sprawled, oblivious to its own good fortune of wealth

1

and mild weather. Eager students crowded the plaza, sharing conversation, enjoying politics and sunshine. Tuition was paid and demonstrations were organized; the student body marched toward enlightenment while administrators measured learning in columns of income and expense. Dr. Ross missed Boston, where even rebels respected the seasons and the cold forced debate indoors.

Nothing in her manner hinted at uncertainty. She set her shoulders stubbornly. The pose of perfect posture had once helped her to look taller. Now maturity added fullness, not height, to her figure. A month of classes had not increased her self-assurance, nor had it altered the determined set of her chin. Soft waves of gray hair saved her profile from an expression too severe. Sandra Ross looked serious as she crossed the plaza.

She hastened up the steps of the history building and through a maze of corridors. Campus lore credited the building's unusual floor plan to two quarrelling architects, brothers who had sacrificed structure to sibling rivalry. The erratic result was a nightmare to newcomers and those late for class.

A handwritten card announced Dr. Ross and her office hours. A student leaned against the door in disregard of the appointed hours.

"Dr. Ross? I wonder if I might have a moment of your time?"

Sandra frowned, then gave a mental shrug. She would remind the student later of her schedule.

Unlocking her door, she said, "Come in."

One long window rescued the room from claustrophobia. A California live oak dominated the panes with downward sweeping branches. Beneath the

2

tree, a plain wooden bench bordered a patch of grass. The interior of the office was a simple matter of desk and shelves losing a battle of space with books and papers. The new doctoral diploma had yet to be unpacked, as if hanging it on the wall would announce publicly a course of action still privately in doubt.

Sandra walked around her desk and considered the window. The oak held carefully to its leaves, impatient eavesdroppers crowding the glass, trying to save themselves from the impending winter's silence. The live oak's grayish-green leaves would not fall. After only a month in Berkeley, she no longer anticipated an inspired burst of color. Watching the season pass was a matter of habit.

Turning, Sandra saw that her visitor still waited on the threshold. She indicated the chair in front of her desk.

"Have a seat. I'm sorry, I don't recognize you from class, you'll have to help me with your name."

The young woman stretched her legs as she sat down, scraping long fingers through short, dark hair. She hesitated briefly, then spoke with confidence. "Excuse me, Dr. Ross. My name is Jessica Hope. My family . . . everyone calls me Jay. I'm not one of your students. I want to know if you will supervise my historical methods and research project."

Sandra looked at the student whom she had never met and was baffled. "Why have you come to me, Ms. Hope?"

"Please call me Jay. My mother is Roberta Hope, director of the Hope Foundation in San Francisco. My grandfather was Arthur Hope." She rested an elbow against the back of her chair, the relaxed pose

3

at odds with a snapping intensity in her copper-colored eyes. Above the eyes, straight black slashes of brow collided in concentration. When she spoke, her voice was without inflection, as if reciting a well-learned phrase by rote. "Grandfather created the foundation for the preservation and development of the arts and humanities. My family is well-known in academic circles. The foundation donates heavily to universities and museums."

Sandra felt another frown forming. Jay Hope might be a favored child of philanthropists but that did not explain her request. "Ms. Hope . . . Jay." Sandra paused, trying to reframe her question. "You're asking to submit a research project to the history department?"

"Yes."

"And," Sandra persisted, "you're asking me to be your supervisor?"

"Right."

Sandra sat back in her chair, contemplating the request. Research projects, she knew, earned advanced academic standing, enabling talented students to graduate ahead of schedule. An instructor's recommendation was crucial, however, and teachers, not students, usually invited a proposal.

Sandra said, "Surely you know a lot of people at the university. There must be other professors familiar with your work, instructors more qualified to give you supervision."

Jay tapped a booted foot impatiently. "Doctor, I came to you first because you're the only one who doesn't know me or my family." She said bluntly, "I need a supervisor I can count on for objectivity."

4

Sandra asked calmly, "Will you elaborate on that comment?"

Jay laughed. "You really don't know, do you?" She looked at Sandra thoughtfully. "I'm sorry, Doctor. I'll try to be specific."

Sandra watched as the rain began, fat drops pushing wet leaves against the window. Jay had explained herself and departed, asking for Sandra's answer as soon as possible.

A large amount of money waited in trust for Jay, an inheritance from her grandfather. The terms of his will would release the funds to Jay on the condition that she earn a four-year, undergraduate degree from the University of California. The Hope family, a clan of insistent academics, had long been disappointed with the bright young daughter who refused to finish college.

"Failed miserably every time I tried," Jay had said. The family, apparently, couldn't decide which was worse — that she lacked a diploma, or that the monies in trust would revert, if Jay didn't comply by her thirty-first birthday, to the National Rifle Association. Grandfather Hope had been an avid hunter.

Sandra crossed her arms, staring at the empty bench outside. Jay would have to complete almost three years of coursework in less than two years, impossible without advanced standing. She also seemed determined to avoid any connection to the family foundation. The estrangement puzzled Sandra.

Perhaps the student merely wanted a professor who wouldn't send report cards home to Mom.

A gust of wind rattled the heavy window panes and Sandra frowned at her own cynicism. Jay wanted an undergraduate degree by the time she turned thirty-one. She was twenty-nine and waiting for a response. Students, she supposed, had a right to believe in answers, although Sandra often despaired of providing them. Unfortunately, over the years, too many of her own questions had gone unanswered.

And many of her decisions left her feeling uncertain. She had delayed social protocol for as long as possible, standing by while the ranks of her peers had surrendered to marriage. She had never understood their eagerness, and surprised herself by accepting a husband and his home when she turned thirty. It had been a childless marriage lasting eleven years, leaving her with little but the desire to overcome convention. She didn't realize until it was over that the emotion behind her marriage had been acceptance, not love. Coming out had seemed so obvious. Still, conformity clung to her, wrapping her in unwanted tentacles of doubt. The decision to love women hadn't defeated her fear. Sandra returned to school. Intellectual passion, she discovered, was almost enough to bring peace of mind.

One year, in graduate school, she had knocked on a professor's door, locked in spite of a scheduled appointment. She heard movement but no answer, and knocked again.

"Who is it?"

"Sandra Ross. I have an appointment with Dr. Higgins."

After a long pause the door opened a crack,

6

releasing marijuana fumes into the corridor. Dr. Higgins pulled Sandra inside and provided thirty minutes of insightful commentary on her dissertation while finishing a joint.

"Well," he said as she thanked him, "we'll know soon enough if we got it right."

Sandra was determined to get it right. Except that right and wrong in California seemed as futile as the seasons. Without fall colors to mark the passage of time she felt disoriented, fearful of a winter filled with leaves. Unable to trust the scenery, she searched for more familiar structure.

Sandra remembered her office hours with a start. She should have reminded Jay to respect her schedule. Stepping quickly into the corridor, she tugged at the small card fastened to the door frame. Pulling it free, she set off to find a photocopier, preferably a machine that made enlargements.

# Chapter 2

Sandra couldn't decide if Barry Donovan was droning or whining. She doodled on her notepad. The weekly faculty meetings were a necessary formality. Droning, she finally decided. Barry always sounded whiny.

"I just don't see how we can give our upper-level students the quality education they deserve," he was saying.

Sam Kaplan, the elderly department chair, nodded gravely as Barry said "quality education" for the third time. Sandra made a tick on her notepad. Barry had said "professional responsibility" twice and "deeply concerned" several times — she'd lost count on that one.

"Well, Barry," Sam interjected, "I believe we all share your deep concern."

Sandra looked up as Sam spoke the favored phrase. His eyes flashed to Sandra then back to Barry.

"I know it's a struggle to balance quality education and professional responsibility with limited resources," Sam continued reassuringly. "No one takes that struggle more seriously than you, Barry, and we all benefit from your motivation. In the meantime, I'll see if I can change the schedule for next semester." He turned back to the group as Sandra marked her pad. "Anything else on the agenda for today?"

Sandra said, "I've been asked to supervise a research project."

"I wasn't aware that an invitation had been made."

"This request came directly from the student. Do you know Jessica Hope?"

Sandra's remark met with shocked silence. She braved the circle of stares, waiting for her colleagues to shed their pillar-of-salt impressions. A document awaiting verification, she thought, could not have been more closely scrutinized.

Sam cleared his throat and said slowly, "So, she registered after all."

"I'll review her transcripts," Sandra offered. She hesitated before asking, "Is there a problem?"

"A timely request," Sam said flatly.

Barry Donovan began to gush. "Why, this is

9

wonderful. Her family must be so relieved. It's no secret they were about to give up on her."

Barry was still trying to win a tenured position in the department. He had carved a niche for himself studying cultural documents recovered from Central America. It was a narrow area of expertise, but his initial inspiration had soured to pomposity. He seemed constantly surprised that he could not yet rest easily on his laurels.

Barry smiled. "Pardon me for asking, Sandra, but why do you suppose Jay Hope came to you? Not that anyone doubts your credentials," he rushed on. "It's just that some of us are known to be on good, ah, professional terms with the family."

Sandra smiled back with bright insincerity. "I believe she wanted to avoid professional, ah, complications."

"Of course, of course." He lapsed into self-important silence.

"Well, Sam, what's the procedure in this case?" Audrey Linden went, as usual, directly to the point. A woman of few words, she remained one of the more dynamic speakers Sandra had ever seen. Lecturing on patterns of epidemic disease and population shifts across the Asian continent, she frequently packed university auditoriums. Sandra had heard one of her presentations at Radcliffe. Her looks alone commanded attention — black hair graying to the color of granite, wide eyes reputedly sharp enough to pin a student to a seat with a glance. Elegant and reserved, Audrey favored striking jewelry, dramatic against her black skin. Audrey had earned a master's degree in biology before pursuing doctoral work in history.

Sandra glanced at Audrey appreciatively as Sam answered her question.

"Anyone can petition," he said. "The faculty supervisor usually recommends the completed project, although a paper may be presented independently." He added, "An appointed committee makes the final decision."

"Well, then," Audrey intercepted smoothly as Barry inhaled to speak, "the decision to supervise or not is yours, Sandra, since the request was made of you."

"I'll let you know as soon as possible, Sam."

Audrey commented dryly, "Good luck."

Audrey would take the project in a second, Sandra guessed. Was it a good sign that a researcher who embraced such topics as death and disease would enjoy working with Jessica Hope?

After the meeting, Sam consulted Sandra's notepad. "How did we do?"

"You got 'professional responsibility' and 'quality education,'" Sandra told him. "Extra credit for using them in one sentence. Half credit for 'concern.' You missed the adverb and tense. Nice try with 'motivation' but that was last week's word."

"Thought I could slip it in."

They had been keeping track of Barry's repetitive phrases for a month. The trick was to repeat his exact words. If Barry ever noticed, Sandra thought, he'd probably be flattered.

Sam crossed his arms and regarded Sandra thoughtfully. "Will you take the supervision?"

"Probably." She shrugged. "The idea seems to make everyone nervous."

11

"The Hope family has been making the university nervous for years," Sam said grimly.

Sandra raised her eyebrows at his comment but the chairman was already headed toward the door.

"You can always reach me at home if I'm not in my office," he called over his shoulder.

Sandra followed him out a moment later. Sam's friendship surprised her. In graduate school, she had questioned one of his papers at a Boston conference. He invited her to coffee and their argument continued by mail. When Sandra completed her doctorate, he encouraged her application to the university. Whether or not he intended to continue the mentorship was uncertain; Sam chaired the department from a discreet distance.

Sandra hurried toward her next seminar.

"Dr. Ross." A graduate student pushing long hair out of his eyes caught up with her as she entered the classroom. "About last week's reading . . ."

Sandra pushed her own tangle of thoughts aside, giving herself over to the questions, arguments and insights of education.


At the end of the day, Sandra dropped her shoulder bag, heavy with notebooks, onto an extra chair in the noisy café. Amy Greenburg was already sipping coffee from a tall glass.

Long established in the psychology department, Amy had befriended Sandra at a function for women faculty. "I already know everyone else," she had declared by way of introduction. A native of Berkeley, Amy breathed its idiosyncracies like a fish extracts oxygen from water. She was at least a dozen years Sandra's junior but frequently confessed to a lot more life experience.

"You look exhausted, dear. Go get yourself something strong."

"Heavy books build strong minds and muscles," Sandra quipped.

"That's what the back seats of cars are for," Amy added. "Carrying burdens." She smiled. "Among other things."

Sandra preferred public transportation to the hassle and expense of city driving. Berkeley, to her delight, had an excellent system. She waved aside Amy's teasing and pushed her way to the counter. The café was just far enough from campus to escape a glut of students. The fact that it was overrun with liberal and contented professionals couldn't be helped. Successful with their skyline view, they raised healthy families in the hills overlooking the bay.

Sandra had considered a few apartments in those expensive neighborhoods but settled in the end for what locals called the flats. She felt more comfortable with the perspective of hills above rather than below her, and the proximity of city streets appealed after the confines of campus. Sandra claimed a mug of coffee and rejoined Amy.

"So, what's on your mind?" Her plump features showed concern as Amy patted a sleek haircut into place. "I think your frown lines are deeper."

"Are you familiar with the procedures to petition a department for advanced standing?"

"If you're looking for a promotion, dear, you might want to wait until after your first semester."

Sandra grimaced. She was not eager to invest

herself in department politics. "I've been asked to supervise a student's research project."

Amy looked up from her coffee with surprise. "Already? Do tell, who's the crash victim?"

Sandra set her cup carefully on the table. Amy had a way with idioms. A crash referred to a student-teacher crush, and Sandra wasn't sure she cared for the imagery.

"I rarely doubt your assessments," Sandra allowed, "but I just met the young woman today. Have you heard of Jessica Hope?"

Sandra expected a reaction. Amy, after all, had spent most of her life in Berkeley. But she was mildly alarmed when Amy sat perfectly still for a long minute. The Hope family seemed to have Medusa-like powers. Finally, Amy said quietly, her voice humorless, "Does Sam Kaplan know?"

"Yes, I told him." Sandra was puzzled. "Do you know Sam?"

"The Kaplans and Greenburgs are old friends." Amy hissed, "I can't believe he's going to let this happen."

"Let what happen?"

"Stay away from that family, Sandra. I'm not kidding. They play with fire."

"Amy, what do you know about them?"

Amy shook her head, clearly trying to reclaim her humor. "That's it. Get a fire extinguisher for your office and make sure your exits are clear."

Sandra tried to dig further but Amy just smiled into her coffee.

"One of the persistent rumors about Jay Hope is that she's gay."

Sandra said mildly, "Surely that's not what makes everyone so uncomfortable."

"It doesn't make me uncomfortable in the least." Amy's smile threatened to become a grin. "And you, dear?"

Sandra laughed at the obvious prying. "I'm not secretive. I knew I was gay before I began my graduate work."

"So what are you waiting for? San Francisco is overflowing with eligible women. I'll help you find them."

"You had me convinced you were straight," Sandra said, stalling Amy's questions.

Amy sighed. "In practice if not in spirit. It's a damn shame, too. Lesbianism is so chic these days." Amy finished her coffee and stood. "I've got to run, but I'll be happy to loan you my map of the women's bars. In the meantime, stay away from Jay Hope."

Sandra watched Amy disappear down the street, to find her car and head for her home in the hills, and probably a hot tub, Sandra thought, completing the Berkeley scene in her mind. She had no doubt that Amy would, if asked, guide her through the avenues of local gay culture. She tried to smile but gave up, frowning fiercely instead.

The richness of the Bay Area beckoned. Full of humor and pain, San Francisco was a handsome city. The rest of the country poked fun and then withdrew, shocked to find their fingers bleeding from the sharp facets of change. Sandra admired the city's diversity and beauty, yet she missed her old friends.

A gaggle of customers settled cozily into neighboring chairs. Sandra eyed the new patrons with annoyance. They dressed casually and chatted easily, the West Coast accent dipping into vowels like a hang-glider in soft wind. Long sounds stuck for just a moment in the throat, never a drawl, not in a hurry.

Sandra swirled the dregs of coffee in her cup, her thoughts circling back to Jay Hope. Given the reactions she had seen, it was no wonder that Jay had come to her. But was there really cause for concern? Whatever her colleagues thought of the Hope family, she had no good reason for denying Jay her request. And, if she wanted more information, it seemed she would have to ask Jay directly.

# Chapter 3

The transcripts were lined up neatly across her office desk. A useless effort, Sandra thought, as though laying them out in orderly fashion could help her discern a clear path through a jungle of academic indecision. Jay hadn't exactly failed — to recall her blunt word — so much as neglected to establish a consistent course.

Sandra took off reading glasses and focused on the young woman seated across the desk from her. No wonder she had never earned a degree, Sandra mused. She hadn't stayed in one department long enough.

"Well." Sandra was determined to establish the rules. "Literature and art history can easily be credited toward a history degree, and biology will fulfill general requirements. In fact," Sandra glanced at the records before her, "you won't have any trouble meeting general requirements." She added in spite of herself, "I don't think you need any more poetry classes, however."

Jay sat patiently with an expression more amused than contrite.

Her hands clasped to hide her irritation, Sandra assumed a Barry Donovan pose and addressed Jay in her most professional tone. "I will accept the supervision of your research project, provided you satisfy all requirements. Your work must be above average at all times. I will file your project with the department after receiving an acceptable outline and proposal statement from you. Have them in my mailbox by the end of the week." Sandra consulted her calendar. "We'll discuss your proposal one week from today." Satisfied, Sandra sat back, pleased to see that Jay now regarded her without any hint of amusement.

"Thank you, Doctor," Jay said quietly. "It means a great deal to me that you're willing to take my work seriously."

Jay walked out and Sandra stared at the empty doorway. She looked at the transcripts still neatly arranged before her. They showed a lack of direction, certainly, but no one could deny that the grades were excellent. When had anyone ever failed to take this bright young woman seriously? She was still staring at the transcripts when Barry Donovan walked in.

"I just passed Jessica Hope in the hallway." Barry helped himself to Sandra's extra chair. "You've decided to help her, then?"

"I'll be supervising her research project, yes."

"Good. Great." Barry crossed his legs and stroked one knee nervously with the palm of his hand. "The Hopes are a generous family."

Sandra eyed him with curiosity and vague repulsion. He was younger than her, mid-forties probably. Already his mannerisms had congealed into narrow habits. He reminded her of Jell-O — artificial coloring and a tendency to wiggle. Barry sought status but lacked the guts to find it on his own. A social climber, he molded himself around those whom society had already accepted.

"Well." He gave Sandra a saccharine smile. "I guess you're the lucky one."

"Why am I lucky, Barry?" Sandra gathered Jay's transcripts and stacked them in a file.

Barry hopped out of the chair and let his hip flow over the side of her desk.

"Come on, that family funds research like millionaires buy stock. If you play your cards right, you'll be golden."

"Have you submitted a proposal for funding?" Sandra asked.

"Not yet. They're highly selective. It helps to have, ah, recommendations, you know, from those already funded."

"Ah, recommendations." Sandra picked up a pencil and scored herself a point, counting his phrases automatically.

"So, what do you say about dinner? I'm happy to fill you in on what I know about the foundation."

"Dinner? Barry, thank you, no."

He pushed himself away from the desk with a shrug. "Hey, just give a holler if you get in over your head. I'll bail you out if it's not too late."

"If it's not too late," Sandra said with a tight smile, "I'll holler for you to bail."

She bit her pencil as Barry sauntered off. How much extra credit, she wondered, for a bad pass?

By Friday afternoon, Sandra wanted to scream at the next person who mentioned Jay or the Hope family. While the foundation was referenced in hushed tones, faculty freely traded speculation about the renegade daughter rumored to be everything from a reclusive genius to a reckless failure. Sandra shoved the rest of her files into her shoulder bag, turning as Jay Hope walked in.

"You're smaller in real life."

Jay said, "I beg your pardon?"

"I've heard a few tall tales about you this week."

Jay's eyes sparkled when she laughed. "Who are they betting on, me or the NRA?"

"Actually, no one seems to know about that part. I think you dashed a lot of hopes, so to speak, when you asked me to supervise."

"And look what I got," Jay said with a smile.

"Objectivity and integrity, too. Why didn't you say anything about the money?"

"It didn't occur to me that it was anybody's business. Is it your primary motivation?"

"No," Jay answered firmly. "It's not." She handed a folder to Sandra. "My outline."

Sandra placed it in her bag. "Our appointment is next week."

Jay looked steadily at Sandra. "Thank you, Dr. Ross." She added, "You're very nice, in real life."

Jay really was rather tall, Sandra noticed, watching her stride down the corridor. Sandra locked her office and headed for the bus stop.

The ride home seemed longer than usual. Rain threatened and retreated, then drizzled indecisively. It was too early in the semester for her to feel so tired. Jet lag no longer counted as an excuse for the insomnia. Maybe she should find a new hobby. Better yet, maybe she could find something to write about, a condition of her employment which had so far defied her best pencil-bitten efforts. The words that had always come so easily in Boston seemed to melt in warm air like spring snow.

Light rain slapped her shoulders as Sandra walked the last blocks to her small house at the edge of the Berkeley hills. A tiny entryway led into a large front room that doubled as both living room and study. Sandra preferred house plants to pets but had yet to decorate thoroughly. Her one extravagance, a coffee-colored leather sofa, faced a sliding glass door. A big wooden desk occupied one wall where a second chair might have stood. Beyond the glass door, an inviting deck gave way to sheltering hills.

The view of the Berkeley hills had enticed her to rent the house. Winding firetrails, used by joggers and hikers, crisscrossed the terrain, providing breathtaking vistas of San Francisco and the Golden Gate. Bay Area natives, no doubt, would think it odd that she preferred to watch the hills.

She'd been amused when a recent article in the campus paper described the off-trail adventures of an unfortunate biology class. To the surprise of their professor and the aggravation of the campus health center, the young scientists had conducted their first field experiments in a patch of poison oak. She smiled, thinking about it. The dangers in the hills didn't disturb her; she was always careful.

Sandra left the living room in darkness, turning on the kitchen light instead. She favored the kitchen in her new home almost as much as the hillside view. Opening off of the wide front room, the kitchen covered more square footage than her bedroom. As far as she was concerned, it was an appropriate apportionment of space. Cooking helped her stop thinking, and thinking was what she tried not to do when she couldn't sleep.

The only problem with her living space was the lack of a basement, a common oversight in California homes. It left her no place to store the wine. Several racks covered the kitchen counters. Cases were stacked in the spare bedroom next to books waiting for shelves. She planned to set up the extra room as a study; in the meantime, papers spent as much time on the sofa as they did at her desk.

Sandra usually worked intently into the evening, commenting on student papers and researching class notes. Tonight, she struggled over the outline that merely inspired anxiety. She knew she'd given in to sleeplessness when she had the cable hook-up moved into the bedroom. A glass of wine and the remote control kept her company long after the day's lesson plans were put away.

She had tried to throw anxiety out with the packing boxes but somehow it slipped back inside. Perhaps she should have kept the boxes. The West Coast job offer had come more quickly than expected and the choice, at the time, was easy. Now she missed familiar East Coast clutter.

New England claimed its history, California claimed the sun. One made a religion out of seasons, the other, content to leave snowfall far away across a valley, relaxed with the confidence of imminent salvation. Never an optimist, Sandra found it hard to have faith in a new life in a state where nothing died. What was the point of spring when winter remained forever green?

"Everything green dies around here during summer," Amy had advised.

"Wait till the summer drought."

Instead, Sandra waited for sleep in front of the late-night movie. Sipping wine, she envied the bloodsucking vampires who retired to their coffins at dawn for well-earned rest. Coffins, she knew, were a damn sight too easy.

# Chapter 4

On Saturday, when Sandra opened her eyes, the rain had lifted its autumn siege. Sleep, apparently, had not entirely escaped. Hills reclined lazily in the sun but she was in no mood to lounge in bed. Restless, she tossed the blankets aside. She scanned the newspaper quickly over coffee and rifled through the files on her desk. The work could wait, she decided. Heading for the bus stop, she shrugged into a windbreaker.

The northbound bus climbed steadily to the far

side of campus. "Visit the rose gardens," the locals insisted, and Sandra understood why as soon as she stepped off the bus. Sculpted into the hillside, fragrant blossoms welcomed the day's warmth in open exuberance. Even the ever-present skyline across the bay looked freshly washed and starched. The water billowed like a brilliant sheet; the campus remained self-contained, heedless of the tide pulling at its edge.

Sandra found a bench in the sun and paused, watching the bay. Odd that it would seem so foreign; she had grown up by the water. Her brother still lived on Cape Cod. As children they had played for hours, happily exploring the shoreline, unconcerned with the force of waves or the strength of tides.

Couples zigzagged like bees through flowers, alighting to exclaim over the late blooms. Others meandered a more solitary course. The bench beside her creaked and Sandra found herself smiling at Dr. Audrey Linden.

"Beautiful day."

"I thought the rain would never end," Sandra said.

Audrey sat quietly, taking in the view. Sandra searched for casual conversation with this formidable woman.

"Do you come here often?"

"Quite often. I haven't seen you here before."

"This is my first visit," Sandra admitted. "It's lovely."

"Temperamental flowers, roses. I used to grow them but I tired of the fuss."

"What do you grow instead?"

"Rocks." Audrey explained, "I have a rock garden.

The real reason I don't grow roses anymore is that they all died of some dread plant disease. I need a hobby where things don't die."

Sandra laughed at this unexpected revelation from the reticent professor.

Audrey studied the bay with unforgiving concentration. "You inspire confidence, don't you, Dr. Ross? I don't like to admit that I gave up on my flowers."

"As long as we're making admissions," Sandra offered, "I can tell you that I was dubious about moving out here. Knowing that you were on faculty was a strong pull. I think I've read everything you've ever published. I've admired your work for years."

"Jay Hope was in one of my classes back, oh, a couple of years ago."

Unsurprised by the topic shift, Sandra asked, "Would you have supervised her project?"

"No."

"Then I guessed wrong. I thought she would impress you."

"She does impress me."

"Why refuse?"

"Her talents are wasted," Audrey said bluntly.

Sandra struggled to put the harsh words into context. She said cautiously, "Jay lacks focus, perhaps, but as a student she shows promise."

Audrey snorted down the length of her prominent nose. "Jay's playing games. This project is a waste of time."

"Why didn't you say something when the subject came up at faculty meeting?"

Audrey focused a laser-like stare on Sandra. "You're right. Had I wished to object, I should've done so at the appropriate time. My apologies."

"I've already agreed to the supervision."

Audrey sighed. "That's unfortunate."

"How so?" Sandra's vague sense of concern returned.

"As I said, her talents are wasted."

Sandra said slowly, "I can't believe that intellect is ever wasted when applied toward knowledge." When Audrey didn't respond, Sandra searched for easier conversation. She asked, "What are your other interests, besides roses . . . or rocks?"

"A very good question." Audrey rose gracefully from the bench. "I look forward to getting to know you better, Sandra. Enjoy the day."

Later, as she walked down the hill toward campus, Sandra pondered Audrey's remarks. Cryptic comments about the Hope family were both frequent and frustrating. Amid the crowd of Saturday shoppers, Sandra browsed the now familiar collection of ethnic eateries, wine merchants, health food stores and laundromats, relieved to be back on lower ground. The bay view intimidated her more than she cared to admit.

A tidy brown and white sign caught her eye — "Hope Chest Antiques." The upscale storefront was not what she would have expected for an antiques business. In New England, she had often explored rustic barns but Berkeley lacked the rural flavor she associated with antiques. Frowning, Sandra crossed the street.

The interior of the store showed off an expanse of

polished wood. Carved chairs ringed an ornate card table while love seats reclined invitingly nearby. A silver coffee service graced a tea table and a mahogany sideboard dominated one wall. An elaborate highboy completed the room. Sunlight streamed through the large front windows; ferns garnished a smaller window to the side. The service counter in the back hardly detracted from the impression that a customer had entered a wealthy home from a sophisticated, bygone era.

"May I help you?"

The voice behind her sounded with a familiar timbre and Sandra turned quickly.

Jay smiled. "I thought I recognized you. Welcome to The Hope Chest."

Sandra reflected wryly that in such a crowded community she would have to get used to seeing her students off-campus. Jay seemed at home in the elegant shop, and Sandra wondered if the name of the store was more than coincidence.

"Jay, hello." Sandra voiced her thoughts. "A lovely store. Is it a family business?"

"No, I'm afraid the only businesses any other Hope will admit to are academics and philanthropy. I bought this place three years ago after investing tuition money in the stock market. That's when Grandfather stopped speaking to me. The whole point of his fortune was to be able to give money away. Charitable, self-righteous old goat."

Sandra laughed. Jay's eyes held amusement and something else. Sandra tried to look again but the expression flashed and disappeared. Sandra made her living reading documents, not people, but she thought she recognized a familiar shadow around the copper laughter in Jay's eyes.

She remembered Jay's words — *Thank you for taking my work seriously.*

"Tell me how you came to create such a beautiful store," Sandra asked, her interest genuine.

"I used to work for an auction house. The family passions for museums and art history didn't hurt me, of course, but I really learned the trade, dirt, glamour and details, at the auctions." Jay gestured to the room. "I borrowed the layout from the more successful furniture dealers. Let people see how things are meant to look, never trust the customer's imagination."

Sandra couldn't hide her amusement. "And does your strategy work?"

"Like a Midas Touch," Jay admitted with pride. "Some customers still want to find hidden treasures in a junk shop, but decorators bring their wealthy clients here. I can live with that trade."

"Surely a family of art historians wouldn't be able to resist such beautiful classics?"

The fleeting shadow glimmered again in Jay's eyes but she answered with candor. "I won't pretend it doesn't hurt. I almost didn't make it through my first year because my mother actively tried to keep customers away. But not all of the nouveau rich are lapping at the feet of Family Hope. The current running truce is that I don't show my business card at family gatherings."

Sandra remembered Amy's cautionary statements about playing with fire. Jay, for one, seemed eager to face the family flames. A low chime above the door sounded an entrance. An exquisitely tailored, middle-aged man walked directly to Jay, bending to give her a kiss on the cheek. Jay made introductions.

"Jonathan, may I please introduce Dr. Sandra Ross, newly appointed to the department of history at the university. Sandra, Jonathan Blake, my assistant and long-time friend."

Sandra smiled at Jay's formal introduction and shook his hand.

Jay added affectionately, "Jonathan recently sold his own design business and retired, but he couldn't keep his nose out of the kitchen."

Jonathan addressed Sandra with a solemn expression. "This young woman took me in and saved me from an old age full of boredom and despair. Her charity knows no bounds."

"Charity, my ass." Jay laughed. "This old fart almost single-handedly saved my business during the first-year drought of Hope. I owe him."

Entertained, Sandra turned away while Jay and Jonathan excused themselves to discuss business. Jay, however, returned in a moment.

"Jon's watching the store for the afternoon. Have you had lunch?"

"Lunch sounds great."

She struggled to remember that familiarity with students was a subject she normally guarded herself against as carefully as she planned her office hours. That the professional young woman before her was not a typical student was as obvious as it was a useless excuse. Sandra tried to dismiss her inner debate. She liked Jay.

They ate fluffy omelettes with homemade salsa and fresh fruit, accompanied by endless cups of strong coffee. Jay talked about antiques, knowledge sparkling in her eyes.

"Every piece has a story, a reason for ending up in my shop. Someone didn't care for the family heirlooms, someone else loved their trinkets but needed money. Ownership generally has nothing to do with the value of an antique, but I'm always curious."

"Jay, you really are an historian."

"Be careful, Doctor, you'll have me running to the foundation for a grant." Jay spoke mockingly, but her eyes turned serious.

So changeable, Sandra thought, like a New England thunderstorm. Ravaging, over in an instant, easy to forget if you weren't soaking wet. The fleeting glimpse of emotion disappeared again but Sandra was starting to watch for it, like looking for lightning while the sky was still clear.

"Jay," Sandra asked quietly, "why do you resist academics so much?"

"Because I never felt like I fit."

"Everywhere I turn on this campus I meet another activist group or political organization. Surely there must be a few kindred spirits."

Jay leaned into the table on crossed arms. "I've opened my checkbook to my share of causes. I'll be honest, though, the last time I went to a demonstration I came home with a headache. At the end of the day I find poetry more inspiring, and less tiring, than politics. How about you?"

"I guess I'm a true introvert." Sandra smiled. "I prefer to analyze my politics in quiet company."

"Maybe I should reconsider my kindred spirits," Jay murmured.

Feeling unexpectedly exposed, Sandra sat back in her chair, trying to cover her emotions.

"As for academics," Jay's tone returned to playful sarcasm, "my family views the university as a sort of elaborate finishing school. I was given a choice of careers from the basket of family gems. All I have to do is find polish and bring the jewel home for display."

Sandra sipped her coffee. "You make it sound like the English royalty should be complaining."

Jay laughed. "I don't deny my privilege."

"Won't your family accept the other, successful choices you've made?"

Jay's eyes flared brightly. The pain was back and Sandra leaned forward, unwilling to let the storm slip away again.

"My family has branded me a failure," Jay said quietly. "Their blame casts a long shadow and I'm tired of cringing in corners to avoid the chill. I'm taking the fight to them."

"Is it a fight you can win?"

"Maybe, in terms of peace of mind." Jay shrugged. "If I get the damn degree it might be easier to walk away."

"Conquer the past before you embrace the future?"

"Something like that."

Sandra set her coffee cup aside. She wondered when she would be able to stand on the beach without feeling the press of waves between herself and the horizon.

"You always look so serious." Jay's words teased gently.

"Tell me why you decided to pursue a history

degree," Sandra asked, eager to shift the conversation.

"You're the newest professor on campus." Jay grinned. "I checked. What made you decide to supervise my project?"

"Because in spite of all your talk about trust funds, I think you're serious about learning."

Jay regarded her thoughtfully. "You get right to the heart of things. That must be useful to a researcher."

Sandra reached for the check. "I always seem to raise more questions than I can answer."

Jay walked with Sandra to the bus stop, embracing her quickly, cheek against cheek, before disappearing into the crowd. Sandra touched her fingers to her cheek, pressing against a warmth that dissipated quickly.

"Well, professor," Sandra mocked herself. "How do you interpret this bit of information?"

Her fingers grew cold and she shoved her hands into the pockets of her windbreaker. Jay Hope was charming. Also smart, successful and unhappy. Sandra sucked in a breath at the unwelcome thought. Jay wanted to prove herself, that was all. Emotional motivation was neither Sandra's area of expertise nor her concern.

Sandra fidgeted in her seat as the bus made ant-like progress down the crowded avenue, veering sharply at each stop to disgorge or ingest bits of busy human life. The need to prove oneself was a heavy burden. Conformity carved a trail, scorning the incautious who wandered out of bounds. She would have to be careful. Jay Hope defied form, and Sandra needed form very much.

The bus followed a course around the campus. The doors popped open and closed, fares were paid and futures approached, stop by stop. Campus buildings crouched at the edge of the bay, a cemented line of giant insects caught in the posture of progress. Impenetrable armor protected the secrets of success; the sharp fangs of failure always threatened. They were all bitten in the end, injected with the venom of need, made to crave the flavor of fulfillment. Sandra had no answers to absorb the pain. Self-acceptance was an effective salve; it was also expensive medicine.

The sun disappeared behind a cloud and Sandra shivered as she walked the last block home. She ran quickly up the low steps to her porch and hurried inside. She took a deep breath and shrugged out of her jacket, shaking herself to dispel the chill of her own mental wandering. Brief daylight remained and the hills beckoned warmly through the window. Sandra stood watching them, absorbing their steady presence as they would soon absorb the last light from the setting sun.

# Chapter 5

Sandra tapped her desk, first with one end of an unsharpened pencil, then the other, unwilling to admit her irritation. Jay's proposal outline lay before her. There had been no sign of her in more than a week. She briefly considered contacting her at her store but discarded the idea in frustration. That Jay should miss her first supervision meeting was simply unacceptable.

The outline itself was fine, the methodology clearly detailed. "The Development of Dueling in European Society." An unusual topic, and too large.

Research would have to be narrowed to a specific period. Sandra wondered if Jay would produce actual swords for her final presentation. A presentation which was already in jeopardy.

"Damn."

Sandra swore out loud and pushed the outline aside. Why the hell should she care if Jay sabotaged herself again? Excellent work with no follow-through, that seemed to be the pattern. It was because the work was excellent that she had let herself become invested.

Another, more uncomfortable concern pushed itself forward. It wasn't her job to provide Jay with the accolades and laurels the Hope family withheld. Sandra clenched her jaw. Jay had come to her for help, and damned if she wouldn't try to give it. She left the outline on her desk and headed outside, thinking that a walk would do her good.

Clusters of students congested the campus. Sandra brushed past nylon backpacks, lazy conversation in the air. The rain continued its truce and clear weather prevailed. Cold sunlight flashed in laughing copper eyes.

Sandra chose a flank attack and marched in from the side to interrupt. Jay's eyes continued to laugh although she turned and stepped away from the animated discussion. The other students, none of whom Sandra recognized, wandered away, voices sounding staccato points across the plaza.

"You missed our scheduled meeting. My regular office hours are posted. Make sure you come in this week."

The laughter vanished from Jay's eyes but she said nothing. After a moment of silence Sandra turned away. She took a few steps, then paused to look back. Jay stood quietly with no expression.

"Your outline, by the way, is excellent."

Sandra returned to her office, reordered her thoughts and collected her seminar notes. She bought coffee in a paper cup and carried it to class. Half a dozen other cardboard containers littered the conference table. Amy had laughed when Sandra mentioned insomnia, suggesting decaf. Sandra consulted the contents of her cup. If she couldn't sleep she may as well enjoy staying awake.

Students settled into seats. Sandra turned to an energetic young woman with curly dark hair.

"Rachel, you're presenting today."

The seminar covered religious influence in medieval society. Rachel opened a notebook and began to catalogue Joan of Arc's campaign at the siege of Orleans. Claiming heavenly guidance, Joan had inspired the prince and rallied his troops, turning back the English onslaught in the Hundred Years' War. Manny, with the long hair, fired the first question.

"Why is she so believable? The prince is seeking a divine symbol and the army wants leadership. How can she be at once pure and convincing to fighting men?"

"Separate myth from fact," Sandra suggested. "What do we know of her character from historical narrative?"

"By all accounts, she really was a virgin," Rachel reported. "That fact alone seems to have inspired a good deal of myth."

"Why is virginity inspirational?" Manny demanded.

"A fine question, indeed," Sandra allowed, to

laughter from around the table. "Narrow the focus. Why, specifically, do so many accounts go to such lengths to document her virginity, and how is that fact perceived, given the religious beliefs of the period? And —" Sandra looked around the table as students scribbled notes — "what place does religion occupy in the lives of fighting men?" She paused. "Arguments?"

The students argued back and forth for an hour. Sandra relaxed, letting the discussion flow around her. It amazed her that the form of history changed so slowly, if at all. Virginity, she imagined, still inspired, although, like Manny, she often wondered why. And religion persisted and the world still asked to be saved.

Her own research documented changes in the Church of France during the first half of the fourteenth century. The role of religion in common life was an issue to which Sandra returned time and again in fascination. The Church offered organization when politics often produced only chaos, and salvation softened the harshest reality. Sandra relished the inconsistencies of a century where chivalry warred with savagery and life courted heaven and hell with equal fervor. She remained impressed by the gap between moral ideals and grim daily practice, and had long ago reached the conclusion that the Middle Ages deserved more credit for civility, while modern society was far more barbaric than anyone cared to admit. She also readily agreed that she herself was untouched by the supreme spirit she researched so thoroughly. She didn't believe in divine intervention. She considered this personal flaw to be either a tragic twist of fate or merely a minor academic point, depending on her mood.

Her mind moved forward a century to join her class with Joan. A color plate in a text caught Sandra's eye — Joan of Arc in armor, a sword belted at her waist. Thinking of Jay, she wondered at her choice of topic. Sandra knew little about the history of weaponry but Jay's outline piqued her interest. Jay's study habits, on the other hand, did not inspire.

The class debated Joan's military strategies versus her visions. Successful at Orleans, she had been captured by the Burgundians at Compiegne. Sold to the English, she refused to renounce her voices or male clothes. For this she was found guilty of insubordination and condemned to death at the age of nineteen.

Sandra found it admirable that any nineteen-year-old could hold such convictions, divine intervention notwithstanding. She thought again of her own decisions. No one could argue with the strategy of a career move, but if certainty were heaven-sent, Sandra remained a heretic. She kept waiting to find direction in a landscape that scared her.

With a reminder about next week's reading, Sandra found another cup of coffee and returned to her office. At three o'clock precisely, she looked up to a knock at her door.

She called, "Come in," and Jay was standing in the doorway.

Sandra allowed herself a moment of satisfaction. Her posted hours for the day were three to five. At least Jay could be prompt.

Setting aside her reading glasses, she said, "Please sit down."

"I apologize for missing our meeting."

"May I ask why you did?"

Formality, Sandra knew, could be a professional courtesy or an academic yardstick of distance. She and Jay might reach comfortable ground if they could navigate the traditional obstacles between work and friendship.

Jay said abruptly, "I usually experience professors as hurdles rather than guideposts. We got off to such a fast start that I had to stop and ask myself if I really mean to do this."

"What did you decide?"

"It would be a shame to waste a good outline."

Sandra recognized an argument's retreat. "Jay, I'm willing to work with you. But I would like to know now if you intend to finish this."

Jay sat silently. "I apologize again," she said finally. "You scare me. It's hard to believe that you really do intend to help."

"I'll help, Jay. What are you going to do?"

"Since you're holding the stopwatch, I think I'll run like hell." Jay's smile did not quite cover the determined set of her mouth.

"I don't think he would have been surprised." Sandra made the statement almost to herself.

"Who?"

"Your grandfather. He must have known that you would excel."

"He just wanted to make sure that whatever I did was on his terms." Jay looked restlessly around Sandra's office. Her fingers found an edge of Sandra's desk and she stroked the wood with her thumb. "I don't want the money."

"What will you do with it?"

"Give it to the foundation, I guess. The NRA isn't my favorite charity."

"Jay!" Sandra exclaimed as understanding dawned. "You're going to buy them off!"

"I think," Jay said evenly, "my motives have changed. I would hate for you to think of me as a failure."

Sandra shook her head. "It's no good, Jay. You can't buy acceptance from me, either."

"I thought maybe I could earn it."

"You don't have to prove yourself to me in that way."

"What then?"

"I'm going to insist on your best." Sandra smiled. "Still think I'm nice?"

Jay said wryly, "If you can figure out what my best is, you're welcome to it."

Sandra jumped at a sudden, shrill sound. Jay too seemed startled but only for a moment. Reaching quickly into her knapsack, she produced a beeper and silenced the intrusive noise.

"May I use your phone?" Jay was already dialing a number.

After listening intently she said, "I'm on my way."

"An emergency?" Sandra asked, "May I help?"

"Forgive me for running out on you. Jonathan, the man you met at my shop," Jay explained hastily, "his lover's been hospitalized. It's not unexpected." Jay said in a rush, "I'm sorry, Dr. Ross."

"Of course. We'll meet next week."

Jay called from the doorway, "Thanks."

Jay's outline still lay on her desk. Sandra placed it in a folder. Her best efforts on Jay's behalf seemed to snag easily between caution and frustration. If there were other hurdles ahead, Sandra mused, it was going to be a long semester.

# Chapter 6

Sandra stood in the middle of her kitchen and eyed the broom in the corner. A bottle of wine waited patiently on the counter. Broken fragments of a wine glass sprayed the floor, a sharp spiderweb at her feet. Maybe she should try sleeping pills. Pills in plastic, unbreakable containers.

Alix, her dear friend in Cambridge, had once gently suggested Alcoholics Anonymous.

"And do what with all this wine? Someone may as well enjoy it."

"Where on earth did it come from?"

"My inheritance."

Alix crossed her arms against an explanation.

"My father collected wine," was all Sandra said.

Her brother, Brian, still had some cases at the Cape. She'd left part of her stock with Sophie and Alix in Boston. Insomnia had plagued her there, too, but familiarity made it easier to forget the water's proximity. All these bay views in Berkeley made her tense. Sandra figured that thirty cases at half a bottle a night would last about two years. If she wasn't sleeping through the night by then, tenure would go in the trash can with the broken glass.

She took a careful step and reached the broom, then mopped the floor with a damp paper towel to pick up stray splinters. Selecting another glass, she uncorked the waiting Rothschild, the last of the case of Moutons. She should have sold it. One case of this would have bought her a semester.

They hadn't found the wine until her mother died. The storage shed had been quietly paid for, month after month, during all those silent years. Sandra and Brian hadn't even known it existed. Dusty paintings, law books and wine; she had thought it all destroyed. When she opened the boxes, memory, pungent as must, closed her throat until she nearly choked.

She had wanted to make space, to bring each painting out into the light and air, to examine pigment and color in search of clues. But she couldn't contain the swell of fear, couldn't risk a closer examination lest old canvas strain and tear.

She had repacked her father's life, and some of herself, wrapping cartons and memories in layers of tape. Now she toasted the ghosts glass by glass and counted the years bottle by bottle until a fragment of grief ripped at her composure. There had been a few jagged moments now and then. For the most part, she tracked her way across the pain with fair equilibrium, until fear came too close and the night reeked of fermentation.

Sandra carried the bottle and glass to her desk and perused her files. It wasn't even ten. One advantage to her long nights, she reflected, was that she had little trouble maintaining her work load. Of course, time might move more quickly if she could draft her own research paper. Sandra sighed, knowing that to force the issue was useless. She wished she could write as easily as she uncorked a bottle.

The phone rang halfway through a batch of student papers.

"Sandra? I am so sorry to bother you at this hour." Sam's usually steady voice sounded on edge.

"Sam? Is anything wrong?"

"My publisher just called. Some kind of problem with my manuscript. She insists I go to San Francisco tomorrow afternoon. I hate to bother you," he said again, "but can you cover my three o'clock lecture?"

"Of course. Will you leave your notes in my box?"

"Yes, oh yes, thank you."

"Sam?"

"What?"

"You're an expert in your field. Tell the publisher I said so."

Sam gave a loud laugh and his voice regained a measure of calm. "You, Sandra, are a savior. Come by for dinner soon."

Joan of Arc was a saint, she thought, hanging up

the phone. Sandra didn't want to be a savior. She just wanted to get some sleep. She returned to the student papers, wondering if there would be any good vampire movies on cable.

Sam's notes crowded her faculty mailbox in the morning. An attached note suggested dinner at seven-thirty. He appeared in her office, frazzled and distracted, on his way to San Francisco. "I'll be back here by seven. How about I give you a lift?"

"If your students rebel next week, you won't thank me."

"You always underestimate your impact. Just don't destroy all my theories at once."

Sandra preferred the intimate conference room to the challenge of lectures. Facing a large audience made her feel a bit like a Christian awaiting the lions. The tiered auditorium seemed to scream for authority. She felt dwarfed, unable to amplify her thoughts to scale.

She spent an hour and a half addressing the development of American government. Not exactly her area of expertise, but Sam's notes were clear and well-organized. Whether or not she entertained the students, she couldn't tell, but they took copious notes.

Sandra, from a family of lawyers, remained dubious about society's struggle to form laws that could at once protect and enhance the individual. It was no secret that both society and individuals often failed, sometimes to an extreme. When governments came close to crushing rather than serving the masses, Sandra usually attributed the problem to poor balance. Balance, in her opinion, was a very difficult position to maintain. The students accepted her words, some with curiosity or defiance, others with careless disregard. Her expertise and uncertainty were not their concern. Sam returned as promised to drive Sandra to dinner. Sam and Evie Kaplan lived in the hills over Oakland, a neighborhood recently ravaged by fire. New construction was everywhere in evidence as they drove. Sandra marveled again at the tenacity of life by the bay. People risked a lot for a view. She couldn't fathom the desire.

Her classmates had called her a risk-taker when she had challenged Sam's paper but, then as now, she based her comments on firm academic ground. Confident of her own methodology, Sandra exposed ideas with determination. Research served as an emotional lifeline and she clung to it fiercely, twining herself in strands of fact. Still, she felt unprotected against inevitable natural disaster — wildfire, earthquake faults and landslides, the inescapable forces of California life. Perhaps the view was more enticing when one accepted anxiety as a neighbor.

Sam herded her into his home and began to complain loudly about his publisher. "They want me to cut three chapters. Three chapters! Make the print smaller, I told her. She just laughed, said people already read my work with a magnifying glass."

"Tell her you'll cut five if she gives you an advance on them as your next book."

"Ah-hah, a brilliant idea!" Sam danced around his living room, clearly trying to release nervous tension. "Next time I'll do the lecture and send you to the publisher. Speaking of which," Sam grew suddenly thoughtful, "when are you going to start writing?"

Sandra grinned. "When I'm damned good and ready and not a moment before."

"Nothing yet, huh?"

"Nope."

He patted her arm. "It will come."

Evie hosted dinner graciously. Her cooking was terrible.

Sandra picked at dry pot roast and stringy vegetables. Sam polished off two helpings in apparent culinary ignorance. Coffee, at least, was palatable. Sandra carried her cup into the next room while Sam rolled up his sleeves to wash dishes.

A sliding door led from the living room to a balcony. The hills stretched around the house and sloped gently to the water, removing the bay view to a more comfortable distance. Evie appeared at Sandra's shoulder, also carrying coffee.

"Sam won't be long," she said, opening the door and stepping outside. "It's a lovely evening."

The night was indeed warmer than usual. The water held the fog offshore and the air settled quietly without a breeze. One side of the balcony had been enclosed to form a glass-walled porch. Sandra could see an easel, stool and painter's workbench. She caught her breath.

"I fancy myself a painter at times," Evie said, following Sandra's gaze.

"This is a beautiful place to paint."

"It suits me."

Sandra stared at the easel. In her mind she saw her father squeezing paint onto a palette, humming tunelessly as he mixed and spread oil on the canvas.

She had loved to touch the lumpy textures as they dried. She remembered his laughter when she once reached too soon and smeared her fingers with wet paint. He lifted her hand and used her finger instead of a brush, drawing the line of horizon, highlighting the crest of a wave.

"Are you a patron of the arts?" Evie startled Sandra out of her reverie.

"No," Sandra said quickly. "No, I'm quite ignorant about art."

Art had never been a subject she cared to study, filling her course load instead with literature and history. She avoided museums and sought inspiration in the less complicated rows of library stacks.

Evie smiled at Sandra's denial. "No one is ignorant of art. It speaks to us all and each of us is blessed with our own unique expression."

"Does Sam paint?" Sandra asked, suddenly curious.

"Heavens, no." Evie sent strong laughter tumbling down the hillside. "Sam is a writer as, I expect, are you."

"What do you do when you can't get it right?"

"Persist in being wrong," Evie replied seriously.

"Who's wrong?"

The women turned at the sound of Sam's voice.

He beckoned, "Come inside for brandy with your philosophy."

Sandra moved back to the safety of civilization. Art and inspiration seemed random dangers. She felt them threaten wildly, like the view, enticing her to an edge she was unprepared to face. She stepped inside and pulled the sliding door firmly shut.

Evie excused herself as Sam and Sandra talked

shop. They discussed courses and articles, arguing interpretations, fighting mock battles on friendly ground.

"Well," Sam said, "you haven't wasted any time getting your feet wet, have you?"

"Actually," Sandra admitted with a smile, "I'm trying very hard to stay dry. I'm a little afraid I'll fall in over my head."

"Nonsense." Sam sounded reassuring. "I've had confidence in you from the beginning." He added, "Thank God you got here in time. Jay Hope seems to have taken to you quite well."

Sandra laughed. "You, too? Why is everyone so fascinated by this research project?"

"There's a lot more at stake here than just a degree."

Surprised, Sandra said, "Jay told me about the trust. No one else seems to know."

Sam covered an awkward silence by pouring brandy. He swallowed a gulp before answering. "As an administrator, it's hard not to cross paths with the Hope family." He cleared his throat. "The important thing is that Jay's found a good supervisor."

Sandra wanted to ask about the Hope family but shied away from what she feared might become a personal conversation. Sam held the world at arm's length and Sandra needed to believe that distance could protect her. When Sam began to yawn she quickly found her jacket and offered to call a cab.

"Evie will take you home. She's a night owl."

Evie reappeared wiping paint off her fingers. "I'll be up for hours yet, it's such a beautiful night. I'll be happy to drive you, Sandra."

Sandra stared at her paint-covered fingers before finding her voice. "Thank you."

The car keys looked bright and clean in Evie's stained hands as Sandra followed her to the car.

"Sam mentioned that you supervise Jay Hope." Evie drove better than she cooked, handling the car casually on the steep descent.

"Yes. The Hope family seems to inspire lock-jaw in the most articulate faculty members."

Evie chuckled. Her eyes intent on the road, she said carefully, "Sam lost some important funding a number of years ago. Roberta Hope almost cost him the department chairmanship."

Sandra listened, her attention riveted.

"He approached the Hope Foundation for alternate funding and was turned down. He managed to publish, in the end, but it took a lot longer than he would have liked. When his name came up for the chairmanship, Roberta offered him a grant. When Sam refused, he found his name had been withdrawn from consideration. He was awarded the chair, in the end, but he compromised to get it." She parked the car in front of Sandra's house. "Fortunately, the academic community holds Sam in high regard and, of course, he's so well-published now. He was very happy when you decided to join the department."

Sandra searched for words. "Jay Hope seems to be at odds with her family. I don't know all the details."

"Sam knows more of the history than he's willing to admit," Evie acknowledged. "However, keeping the Hope family happy is now an important part of his job, and that means he makes many compromises." Evie looked at her. "I wanted to tell you because I know that there will be people who try to use your

51

attachment to the Hopes. In my experience, colleagues are not always allies."

Sandra stepped out of the car and watched tail lights disappear into descending mist. The sudden fog unsettled her. She felt caught in its thickness, unable to see clearly.

She went inside, telling herself that Jay hadn't exactly picked the most confident of supervisors. But confidence was what she most wanted to give to Jay — that, and the safe haven of knowledge.

"Not a bad lesson plan," Sandra murmured as she kicked off her shoes.

The only problem was that she couldn't teach what she hadn't yet learned. She sat up later than usual that night, her wine untouched, thinking about artists and allies.

# Chapter 7

The hills looked even greener by the beginning of November. Sandra hurried across the open plaza as rain began to fall. Head down, she ran up the stairs to the history building, nearly colliding with a student in the doorway.

"Sorry." Sandra barely glanced up, impatient to be inside.

"Dr. Ross."

The student failed to yield and Sandra found herself looking into those familiar copper eyes.

"You're blocking the entrance."

Jay laughed and stepped back, holding the door for Sandra.

"Thanks." Sandra smiled briefly, adding, "I don't have office hours today."

"I know what your office hours are."

Sandra gave Jay an ironic glance as she unlocked her door.

"I was afraid I'd missed you," Jay said, placing a rain-spattered folder on Sandra's desk. "These are my research notes. I have too much material and I thought you might suggest a focus. I can stop by again tomorrow."

Sandra considered the thick folder with anticipation. "Come back at the end of the week."

"Thanks."

Jay turned to leave as Sandra asked, "How are Jonathan and his partner?"

"Michael's still in the hospital. It's bad this time."

"Jay, I'm sorry. Have you known him long?"

"I lived in San Diego for a while, that's where we met. I think he knew he was HIV positive even then. He moved to Berkeley, and when I came back he introduced me to Jon."

Sandra looked away. Wind pushed rain in wet streams along the window. What use, she wondered, to catalogue tragedies of the past when there were so many lives at stake in the present. Research allowed distance but it couldn't preclude responsibility.

Jay asked, "Have you lost someone close to you?"

Sandra turned again, surprised to find Jay still standing at the door. "It was a long time ago. One of the problems endemic to historians," she tried for a smile, "is that we live too much in the past. I hope Michael improves."

Jay left and the office seemed suddenly still. The oak tossed with the blowing storm, scraping branches across the glass. Sandra listened to the noise with relief.

Reading glasses rested on a mountain of files as Sandra switched off her desk lamp. Walking easily across the darkened room, she poured a glass of wine and curled herself into the couch. Her eyes adjusted slowly to the quiet shape of hills behind the house. The small deck fell into shadow earlier each day, and sunlight had long since vanished. Never touched by snow, the soft slopes were a faint reminder of the fierce Sierra Nevadas ranging to the east.

These West Coast crazies with their insistence on bay views have it all wrong, Sandra thought. She'd been watching in daily fascination as the low scrub turned surprisingly green with the wetness of coming winter. In summer it would all dry to a dangerous, fire-sparking brown. Now, in dark silhouette, the hills rose reassuringly, silently aloof.

A knock at the door interrupted the quiet. Sandra turned on a light and glanced at her watch. Nearly eight.

Not expecting visitors, she called, "Who is it?"

"Jay Hope."

Startled, Sandra opened the door.

"No posted hours?" Jay smiled from the threshold.

"I don't usually need them at home."

Sandra moved back from the door and Jay stepped inside, glancing around.

"Very nice." Jay nodded. "Warm."

"No antiques, I'm afraid. Nothing Victorian."

"It sells, but I've never been fond of that period."

"What do you prefer?"

"American Empire. It's not very popular. Lots of clawed feet, scrolled arms, extravagant carving. The Empire period in France used wreaths and urns."

"You must be fabulous in a museum."

Jay rolled her eyes. "I lack a formal education, remember? Speaking of education . . ." She smiled. "I didn't have a chance to stop back at your office. Have you read my notes?"

"Oh, hell."

"That bad?"

"Oh . . . no, sorry." Sandra felt momentarily flustered. "It's just that I already hung the professor in the closet for the day."

"Really?" Jay teased, "You mean that studied air of detachment isn't your natural expression? Who would have guessed?"

Sandra laughed and realized they were still standing in the entryway. "Look, your notes are great and I do have some ideas for you. But you shouldn't be here and I shouldn't let you stay," she added awkwardly.

Neither woman moved.

"Oh, hell," Sandra said again.

"Am I interrupting something?"

"A glass of wine and quiet contemplation."

"Pour me a glass of wine, tell me what I need to contemplate, and I'll take my notes and leave you alone."

Frowning, Sandra asked, "Are you carrying a beeper?"

"No."

She led Jay inside, wondering whether the need to educate or simple companionship offered a better excuse. Opportunity was running an even race with common sense. Sandra handed her a glass of wine and a folder of notes. They sat down on the couch.

"I marked your outline into two distinct periods. You're having trouble because you haven't isolated the trends in each period."

Jay opened a notebook and began to write. She consulted Sandra's notes frequently. Her questions became more focused as she organized the material. Sandra watched the process with enjoyment. Jay followed Sandra's reasoning and then built new layers with her own knowledge. Finally, Jay tossed her notebook aside and stretched. She had been scribbling intently for the better part of an hour.

"You're right, of course," Jay said. "It makes more sense to focus on the first half of the seventeenth century."

Sandra collected loose papers. "Concentrate on the historical developments which underlie the social changes you describe. When you can follow several trends and pinpoint their juncture, you will have a thorough and exciting paper."

"Thanks. You're helpful."

Sandra sat back and picked up her wine glass, forgotten during the lengthy notetaking.

"Do you really turn it on and off?"

"What an ambiguous question, Jay. To what are you referring?"

"Being a professor. You seem to love it."

Sandra sipped her wine. "I guess I do. Teaching seemed like the logical step."

"What did you do before?"

"I was a textbook editor. And I went to school for a long time."

"Are you happy?"

"Your line of questioning is becoming more direct."

"I don't mean to intrude."

"I'm not entirely sure yet," Sandra admitted.

"You're an excellent teacher."

Sandra shrugged. "There are risks beyond the classroom I haven't dared take. I admire your approach, Jay. You try all the questions, not just the easy ones." She smiled. "And you're eager to find the answers at any hour, day or night."

Setting her still half-full glass aside, Sandra stood. Jay rose immediately, gathering her papers.

"Thank you again, Dr. Ross."

"Having relinquished the procedure of office hours," Sandra said lightly, "I see no reason to stand on ceremony with names."

Jay walked to the door. As she had done once before at the bus stop, she embraced Sandra quickly, cheek pressing cheek for a moment. "Good night, Sandra."

This time Sandra had no pockets in which to hide her hands. She folded her arms and leaned back against the closed front door. So much for quiet contemplation.

She said aloud, "Oh, hell."

She returned impatiently to the living room but avoided the couch. Instead, she stood before the glass door, the world outside obscured by the lighted room's reflection. She had no objection to friendships between teachers and students. A cup of coffee was common enough. Graduate seminars and professors had been known to share a drink together now and then. Sandra's hand found its way back to her cheek. Giving a glass of wine to a student in her home was quite possibly the least of her worries.

The branches betrayed no hint of movement, holding the morning sunlight delicately between heaven and earth. Sandra leaned against her office window, looking at the empty bench outside. She sighed. If she wanted to contemplate emptiness, better to wait for warm weather when she could sit on the bench instead of staring at it through glass.

The campus relaxed in the quiet lull between midterms and the Thanksgiving holiday. Her own backlog was well in hand and Sandra felt restless. Refusing to turn around, she thought about the messages stacked on her desk. One small envelope nagged silently and Sandra finally gave in and read it again.

*Mrs. Roberta Hope and family request the honor of your presence at the Hope Foundation holiday banquet and benefit.*

Friday night. One week after Thanksgiving. Time, location and a request for response were carefully detailed. Sandra tossed the invitation back on her desk and reached for the phone. Amy's number wasn't included in her message slips but she dialed it first.

"It's about goddam time," the voice on the other end of the phone said cheerily. "Have you received the Invitation of Hope?"

"Yes." Sandra wondered if Hope idioms were common knowledge.

"Good. Where are you?"

"Campus office."

"Really, Sandra, it's Saturday. Do you have to be there?"

Sandra had the morning to herself and said so.

"Come on up." Amy disconnected without further comment.

Amy owned a small house on a high winding street with a postage stamp deck consumed entirely by a hot tub. A glimpse of bay winked happily below. She greeted Sandra with a dose of psychology department gossip, humorous and sometimes scandalous accounts of faculty indiscretions and general foolhardiness. Amy rarely spared even herself.

"I can't believe I didn't have more sense," she wailed as she set out bagels and coffee. "Visiting faculty, my ass. He's not a psychologist. He's a psychopath with video equipment."

"I thought you were just dating."

"Dinner and a movie, sweetheart. That's all I signed up for. Well, it turns out the movie's at his house and he wants me to pose for the camera. I think I broke his lens, I was so mad."

Sandra laughed, waiting for Amy to find her way to the topic at hand.

"So, how's the Hope child?" Amy didn't need prompting. "Rumor has it that she's actually quite bright."

"She is. Her work is excellent."

"I admire you, Sandra."

"Good heavens, why?"

"Let me put it this way," Amy explained. "When you start playing campus politics, after a while you start to feel like a hired gun. Everyone's busy shooting for points and trying not to get hit by stray bullets. Suddenly Marshall Ross comes to town and starts acting like some things are more important than target practice."

"I'm not sure I follow you, Amy. I don't want a career as a marshall."

"That's just my point," Amy insisted. "You don't get drawn in to the fray. You'll come out clean on the other side."

Sandra shook her head. "If this is how you counsel your friends, I can't quite imagine how you interpret dreams for your patients."

"Easy. The patient has to self-interpret. Saves wear and tear on the therapist."

"It seems to me you might try pacifism if you want to save wear and tear."

Amy laughed heartily. "And miss all the excitement? Too much caution is boring. Sorry, dear."

"Speaking of excitement, can I count on you to attend the Hope benefit?"

"I'll be there," Amy said, "wearing my bullet-proof vest. The Hopes always throw their party early, before Hanukkah. And since you'll be in town, why don't you join me for Thanksgiving. My parents always make dinner. I'll drive."

Sandra accepted with thanks.

"Are you kidding," Amy exclaimed. "You don't know what a favor you're doing me. If I show up with you, Mother won't harass me about a date. I divorced a doctor, so, now I should try for a lawyer. Oy vey. Come on, I'll give you a lift back to campus."

As they descended to sea level, Sandra tried to imagine herself dodging bullets. The forces of nature seemed far more dangerous by comparison, and institutions carried their own compelling poisons. The approaching campus, at the moment, looked neither like an insect nor the setting for a gunfight.

Barry Donovan lurked in the hallway outside her office. "Sandra, I'm glad I found you."

Opening her door, Sandra asked, "What can I do for you, Barry?"

"I expect you'll be attending the Hope extravaganza?"

"Yes, I expect I will."

"Excellent." Barry rubbed his hands together. "I've been to several of these affairs. The occasion is always impressive."

Sandra smiled, keeping a mental tally. "I'm glad I'll have occasion to see for myself."

"I saw Roberta Hope at the fine arts gallery just yesterday. That's why I came to see you. She's very pleased with Jay's choice of supervisor."

Sandra eyed Barry cautiously. "I haven't had the pleasure of meeting Mrs. Hope."

She frowned at her poor choice of words. Barry didn't notice.

"Sandra, surely you must know that your reputation precedes you. I took the opportunity to approach Mrs. Hope and put in a good word for you."

Was it her imagination or was Barry talking too loudly?

Sandra took a breath. "Barry, I appreciate your attention to my reputation, but please take me at my word. I have no plans to approach the Hope Foundation, now or at any future opportunity."

"Oh, well, I see. Certainly, that's clear," he blustered. "Well then, I guess I'll see you at the faculty meeting."

Sandra sank into her chair as he left. She and Sam hadn't started the game to be cruel. Using Barry's own words was simply the best way to shut him up.

# Chapter 8

The history library couldn't compete in size with the large building reserved for general reference, but aesthetics favored the historians. Long wood tables spaced with reading lamps formed rows under an elegantly arched high ceiling. Sandra quickly lost herself in the stacks. It took ten minutes for her to locate the volumes she needed. She quickly found an empty stretch of table and began to take notes. Forty minutes later she closed the books and rubbed her eyes.

Standing to leave, her glance fell on a book lying

open at the next table, the page turned to a color plate that showed some sort of sword. Scribbled notes covered the table, their writer nowhere nearby. Curious, Sandra paused to read.

Two-handed swords, popular in the late Middle Ages, had given way to the one-handed rapier. This change corresponded with a decrease in the wearing of defensive armor. Western Europe had favored a straight sword but Turkish invasions during the sixteenth century introduced curved weapons.

Turning a page, Sandra learned that the art of fencing had developed the use of the pointed rapier — a thrusting rather than a cutting blade. Hand-written notes beside the text referenced changes in the political climate as well as civilian customs. Half a dozen questions were also listed. Still too general, Sandra thought, but getting better.

"Give me a break."

A voice spoke in exasperation behind her. Sandra glanced up to see Jay standing over her shoulder.

Jay folded her arms. "Please tell me you didn't come here to check my work."

"Hello, Jay." Sandra flushed. "I'm sorry, I was just passing through."

Jay let her arms fall to her sides, then reached to gather her notes. "I'm about ready to quit. Can I buy you a cup of coffee?"

The wall clock showed five-fifteen.

Sandra said, "I'll buy the coffee, you fill me in on your current research." She added, "Your questions are still too broad."

"Mm-hmm. Wait till you hear the answers."

Jay hefted her knapsack and Sandra followed her out into the early night. She barely hesitated when

Jay suggested supper. They chose a small café a block from campus.

Sandra cupped her fingers around a bowl of soup and watched Jay break the end from a loaf of bread. The insistent West Coast fog took its toll in terms of chill. Mist rolled in off the water and cloaked the day's warmth in dampness.

Inhaling fragrant steam, Sandra asked, "Why dueling? How did you come to select that topic?"

Jay swallowed a mouthful of bread. "I handled a pair of seventeenth-century Spanish blades for an auction. As it turned out, they were trick swords."

"How could you tell?"

"On a cup-hilt rapier, the cup, or hand-garde, is sometimes patterned. The design is usually just for decoration, but on these swords the pattern of one hilt had been altered. The intent was to catch the tip of the opposing blade."

"Did it work?"

Jay laughed. "I have no idea."

"I wouldn't imagine you're the type to resort to such deception," Sandra commented.

"You, Dr. Ross, are very trusting."

"Is there any reason I shouldn't trust you, Jay?"

Jay's eyes went flat. "Are there people in your life that you trust completely?"

Sandra couldn't read Jay's expression. How could she answer honestly? She may as well admit that she didn't entirely trust herself. She said, "I have friends I trust, don't you?"

Jay replied without sarcasm, "I don't trust myself."

Sandra winced at the private thought Jay voiced so easily.

"Hey," Jay said lightly. "Stop frowning. I could probably still produce references."

"How about producing your research draft?"

Jay pushed a familiar outline across the table and Sandra accepted the page as she might receive a gesture of reassurance. She still had faith in the process of learning and she still trusted the purpose of paper and pen.

As Sandra had observed in the library, the notes showed improvement and she said so. She looked up as Jay raised a hand in greeting to someone across the room. Audrey Linden acknowledged them with a nod.

"Now she's a tough one," Jay said.

"An impressive woman," Sandra concurred. "She thinks highly of you."

"Really." Jay's voice was dry. "Last time I spoke to her she told me I was wasting my life."

"I believe wasting your talents was the phrase she used with me."

"Same difference."

"Why would she make such a statement?"

"I made the mistake of showing her my hobbies. Don't ask," Jay said to Sandra's questioning look. "I'm smart, remember? I try not to make the same mistakes twice."

"She's presenting a paper next week," Sandra told Jay. "Would you like to attend?"

"Yes."

Sandra returned her attention to the work at hand. "All right, let's go through your outline." She pushed her soup bowl aside to make room for the papers. "You've concentrated on the combined influences of politics, warfare and social custom.

67

That's excellent." Sandra tapped her finger on the outline. "Here. The conclusions you draw require more supporting detail. You've laid the foundation, now give me evidence. Why, for example, is the government opposed to the practice of dueling? What advantage is gained by those who choose to ignore the law? More importantly," Sandra continued, "put it in context. What other political and social tensions occur in the same period?"

Sandra sipped coffee as Jay concentrated on taking notes. Out of the corner of her eye, she saw Audrey pause at the door to the café. Sandra turned slightly in her chair and then sat motionless, riveted by the expression on Audrey's face as she looked at Jay.

She had seen such a look once before. She would never forget the mixture of anger and grief imprinted on her mother's features at the news of her father's death. Unaware of Sandra's gaze, Audrey abruptly exited.

Sandra realized that Jay had stopped writing and was also staring at the door.

"What happened, Jay? Why is Audrey so angry with you?"

"It's mutual."

"But why?"

"She takes the successes and failures of her students very seriously. I believe I'm one of her biggest failures."

"For God's sake, Jay. What the hell is going on with the two of you?"

"Nothing."

"Nonsense. I may be an historian but I'm not

immune to current affairs. And the tension between you and Dr. Linden is definitely current."

"Dr. Ross." Jay's voice was low and tight in her throat. "Supervise my schoolwork, please. Let's leave social commentary to the news at eleven."

Sandra sat back in her chair, stung by Jay's tone, shocked at her own insistence. "I'm sorry, Jay."

"Forget it." Jay loaded her knapsack and stood. "I'll see you next week."

Sandra collected her jacket and walked to the door. Jay was already gone. Stay on the path, she scolded herself silently. "And while you're at it," she muttered out loud, "try to avoid the land mines."


Sandra found a seat in the small auditorium moments before Audrey began her presentation. Her latest work documented the impact of infectious disease on civilizations with developed agricultural technology. Farming techniques that had resulted in thriving crops and domesticated animals also increased local concentrations of disease-causing parasites.

Audrey skillfully tracked the parallel movements of civilization and disease during the period from 500 B.C. through A.D 1,000. Sandra marveled at the scope of the research as Audrey followed population shifts and climatic conditions throughout the Middle East and China. She listened to the power of her arguments, enjoying the strong cadence of Audrey's voice. She waited afterwards to pay her compliments.

"Walk me back to my office, Sandra."

Sandra paced herself to Audrey's rapid strides, unsurprised when she asked, "How is Jay?"

"I thought she planned to attend your presentation this afternoon. I don't know what's more unusual, that she wanted to come or that she didn't show."

"You like her."

Sandra glanced up, but nothing in Audrey's manner hinted at the expression Sandra had witnessed in the café. "Yes, I do. She's a good student."

"That's what I was afraid of."

"You sound as if you don't want her to succeed."

Audrey reached her office and pushed open the door. Large, by university standards, the room boasted an enviable pair of windows. Sandra turned by habit to study the view.

"Her success will be empty." Audrey sat down behind her desk.

Sandra spun away from the window. "And you've told her this, I imagine."

"Of course." Audrey seemed unperturbed by Sandra's flair of temper.

"Jesus. No wonder she calls professors obstacles. Nothing like a little negative encouragement."

Audrey arched one graceful eyebrow.

Suddenly tired, Sandra leaned against the window frame. "With all due respect, Dr. Linden, where do you get off?"

Audrey rose and moved to stand beside Sandra at the window. She spoke quietly, but Sandra recognized the power behind her words. "Jay Hope has enormous talent. I have been fortunate enough to experience it first hand. But I must respect her silence in that regard. Jay's failure, as she likes to call her lack of a degree, is another matter. Whether or not Jay achieves success has nothing to do with grades. That's why teachers are so unhelpful. We take far too much credit, handing out passing and failing marks as though we have a right to name winners and losers."

"What mistake does a student have to make," Sandra asked softly, "to lose?"

"Knowledge is useless if a student refuses the truth about herself. But," Audrey continued, "since you have agreed to teach Jay in her quest for academic acceptance, I would like to ask a favor."

Sandra listened intently.

"Look past the words. Try to see what she hides in her heart, and if you find it, nurture it." Audrey smiled. "Don't look so astonished, Sandra. Teachers would do well to cherish the dreams of their students."

Sandra stared at her. Earrings sparkled against her skin; the deep gaze blazed with the need to convey knowledge, as though understanding could be branded eye to eye. Audrey seated herself once more behind her desk and steepled her fingers, the unconscious pose of authority further magnifying the message.

Sandra almost laughed. Audrey looked like a preacher, or something worse. In spite of herself, Sandra did start to laugh.

"I'm sorry, Audrey," she said, trying to stop and laughing harder with the effort. "Oh God, I'm sorry. It's just that I don't understand the sermon."

Audrey looked at Sandra and began to chuckle.

Sandra caught her breath for a moment. "Jesus,

Audrey. I spend hours in my religious history seminar trying to convince myself that there's no such thing as divine intervention. Now you want me to save a soul."

The door opened and Sam Kaplan stood staring at the two women. Audrey's chuckle had turned into full, throaty laughter. Sandra wiped tears from the corners of her eyes.

Sam said, "Excellent presentation, Audrey. What's so funny?"

Audrey glanced at Sandra and said, "After all these years, Sam, I finally fell out of the ivory tower."

"You and Humpty Dumpty," Sam replied evenly. "Don't mind me, I'll show myself out." He shut the door as their laughter faded.

"I'm sorry," Sandra repeated, growing serious. "I'm not arrogant enough to try to impact the lives of my students beyond the classroom. As for success and failure, I believe that's a very personal decision."

Audrey laced her fingers, pressing the palms together. She said thoughtfully, "Sam's been trying to expand the department for ages. We were all surprised when the approval finally came through this year." She sighed. "You're a welcome addition, Sandra. Still, I almost wish Jay had never met you."

"You have a history with Jay that's none of my business," Sandra said quietly. She added with a half-smile, "And I don't want to interfere in the secret hobby society."

"Hobbies become a problem," Audrey intoned, "when we confuse them with our real purpose."

Sandra took a few steps across the room and stood with her back to Audrey, trying to ease a sudden tightness in her shoulders. "Have you always been so certain of your purpose?"

"I have been given to my share of indecision."

Sandra whirled, angry again. She snapped, "Then what right do you have to question the decisions of others?"

Audrey leaned back in her chair. "It's not indecision I detest," she answered calmly. "I take exception to fear."

Sandra went to the desk and leaned on it with both hands. "Fear is something I have a great deal of respect for, Dr. Linden."

Audrey's voice was soft. "Then perhaps you and Jay will have a lot to discuss."


Sandra strode off campus and was half-way up the north-side hill before she let herself reflect on Audrey's comments. Audrey possessed no small talent herself and she seemed well-versed in the subject of Jay Hope. Sandra bit her lip in frustration. She had enough trouble burying her own secrets without worrying about those of her students.

Her classes were done for the day and Sandra indulged herself by browsing through a few of the many small bookstores nearby. It was already dark when she turned back down the hill. She stopped suddenly as the question that had teased her for hours resurfaced. Jay had obviously changed her mind about attending Audrey's presentation, but why had she expressed interest in the first place? Giving in to curiosity, Sandra climbed one more block uphill toward the brown and white sign of The Hope Chest.

The shop lights were on and the door unlocked but Jay was nowhere in sight. Door chimes sounded as Sandra entered. An unfamiliar man walked out from the back of the store.

"May I help you?"

"I'm sorry, I was looking for Jay Hope. I'll come back another time."

A door behind the counter opened and Sandra recognized Jonathan Blake.

"Ian, why don't you start closing." Jonathan paused when he saw Sandra. "Forgive me, I didn't realize we had a customer. May I help?" His face looked pale and drawn.

"Hello, Jonathan."

"Oh, Dr. Ross, isn't it? Please forgive me," he apologized again.

"I'm afraid I came at a bad time."

Sandra turned to leave but Jonathan hurried to place a hand on her arm. "I hate to impose. Please, perhaps you could drive Jay home."

Sandra asked with mild alarm, "Is she ill?"

"She's not sick, but I think it would be helpful if someone stayed with her."

"Where is she?"

Jonathan guided her through the door behind the counter into a small office. Jay leaned against the wall, her eyes closed. She cradled a bandaged hand, gauze wrapped haphazardly and stained with red. A carpet had been pushed aside and broken glass swept into a pile.

"Jonathan." Jay's eyes remained closed as she spoke. Her voice sounded weak. "Lock the front door and get the hell out of here. Have Ian drive you. I'll be fine. Take care of yourself."

"What happened?"

Jay's eyes flew open as she heard Sandra's voice. "Oh, shit." Her eyes closed again.

Jonathan said, "We lost Michael this morning. I didn't want to call but she knew when she saw me. She was holding the bottle." Tears filled the older man's eyes. "It was an accident."

Sandra picked up the broom that leaned beside Jay and turned to Jonathan. "I'm so sorry. Please let your friend drive you home. I'll make sure Jay's all right."

The young man Sandra didn't know stepped forward. "The door's locked. I turned the sign and drew the blinds." He called, "Jay? I'll phone you tomorrow."

Jay opened her eyes and Sandra saw an expression of sheer sadness. Jay pushed away from the wall and moved to Jonathan, placing her clean hand on his cheek.

"Don't call. I'll be over in the morning. Ian, make sure he gets some sleep. I'm sorry, Jon. I'm sorry I broke the damn bottle." She kissed him gently and the two men left. Jay sank into a large leather armchair. She looked at Sandra through blurry eyes. "How the hell did you get here?"

"I walked." Sandra still held the broom. "How did you break the bottle?"

"I think I smashed it against the wall."

Sandra began to sweep glass into a dustpan. She felt Jay's hand on her shoulder.

"Please don't."

"Jay, do you need to see a doctor?"

Jay glanced at her hand and swore softly. "I guess I do."

Sandra watched as Jay dialed a cleaning service, a friend to watch the store for a few days, then a doctor.

Sandra said in surprise, "House calls?"

"I'll call on him. I furnished two homes for him. Actually, one for him, one for his ex-wife. He doesn't hold it against me."

"I'll drive you."

Jay's car was an old Dodge parked in an alley behind the store. Sandra shifted gears with a jerk as Jay gave her directions. The doctor met them at the door, medical bag in hand. Sandra winced as she watched him clean and stitch the cut.

"What the hell did you think you were doing?" he demanded.

Good question, Sandra thought. She looked around the expensively furnished room, recognizing some of the style from Jay's store. One piece of sculpture in the corner caught her eye. A functional bookshelf, it swept upward, floor to ceiling, curving and spreading gently like a tree. Sandra imagined that light from the window falling on wood might look like sunlight on branches. She had never seen anything like it.

"Jesus, Jay." The doctor cursed cheerfully as he stitched. "Jack would have my hide if I told him you ruined your hands."

"Ah, Jack, the famous New York cousin. Tell him to come for a visit. I'll sell him some furniture."

Sandra felt suddenly queasy at the sight of the curved needle hovering over Jay's hand. She sat down quickly and closed her eyes.

She heard the doctor say, "Leave the bandage on and keep it clean. Come to my office in a week and

I'll take out the stitches." The voice paused, then asked, "Is your friend okay?"

Sandra blinked to clear her vision and struggled to her feet. "I'm fine, thank you."

The doctor peered at Sandra, then smiled. "Fresh air should help." He showed them out, calling after Jay, "Talk to Jack."

Jay took the car keys from Sandra as they walked to the curb. "Thanks, Sandra. I'll drive you home."

Sandra took a breath and her stomach settled. "How's the hand?"

"Numb."

"All right, Jay," Sandra said as they descended from the hills. "I've heard that you have great talents you waste on hobbies and now a doctor's cousin is overly concerned with your hands. Would you like to fill in the missing pieces?"

"I design furniture. Jack calls every six months from New York to ask me to go into business. He's a well-known artist. I'd probably learn a lot."

"You don't want to?"

"I'm trying to get an education, remember?" After a moment Jay said gently, "I'm sorry. You've been nothing but decent to me, Sandra. I don't mean to be sarcastic. It's been an awful day."

Sandra thought about the sculpture in the doctor's house. Would she find similar furniture at Audrey's? Jay drove slowly, her injured hand propped on the steering wheel. When the car stopped in front of her house, Sandra paused before opening the door.

"Will you be all right, Jay? Is there someone you can call?"

"I'll be with Jonathan tomorrow. Thanks, I'm

fine." She asked as an afterthought, "How was Audrey's presentation?"

Sandra smiled in spite of herself. "Her paper was most impressive."

"Audrey always argues impressively. All that poise."

Sandra tried to keep her voice light. "I have no intention of walking that minefield again. I must say, though, you're not an easy subject to defend."

Jay looked tired. "You're a saint. But I don't need defending."

"Believe me, I'm no saint." Sandra knew she was keeping Jay. "Did you know that Audrey has a rock garden?"

"She grows roses."

"Not anymore."

"She loves to watch things bloom. She told me."

And she hates to watch things die, Sandra thought. Jay slumped against the car door, her eyes half closed.

"Jay, did the doctor give you anything for pain?"

"Hmm?" Jay roused herself. "Oh, yes, some pills. I think I took one."

"Lock the car," Sandra directed. "Come inside." She reached across Jay's lap and pulled the keys out of the ignition.

"What are you doing?"

"Saving the residents of Berkeley from you behind the wheel of a car. I shouldn't have let you drive this far."

Jay looked as if she might protest further but shrugged, her shoulders slumping again in exhaustion. She mumbled, "I'll take the couch."

Sandra left Jay in the front room while she went

in search of sheets and a blanket. She left an extra towel in the bathroom and returned to find Jay already asleep, one booted leg on the leather couch. Sandra hesitated, unwilling to wake her. After a moment, she unfolded the blanket and spread it carefully, wondering whether or not to remove the boots.

*Who's the crash victim?*

Sandra stood very still, hearing Amy's words in her mind. She looked at Jay, intelligent copper eyes curtained behind closed lashes, sarcasm silenced behind soft lips. Sandra wrapped her arms around herself in an effort to still an involuntary shudder. The abrupt shock dissolved into confusion. Sandra whirled and fled for the bedroom. Jay could take off her own damn boots.


Sandra managed a few hours of sleep, waking before her alarm to the smell of coffee. Pulling on a robe, she walked into the kitchen. "Good morning. How did you sleep?"

Jay handed her a mug of coffee. "I seem to have slept in my boots. I hope I wasn't awake long enough to embarrass myself further."

"You did sort of collapse. How do you feel now?"

"Ragged, but I think I'll forgo the pain pills for a while."

The morning paper lay folded on the counter. Sandra perched on a stool, trying to reclaim her routine.

Jay spoke into the silence. "Thank you for going out of your way, Sandra. I'm sorry I had to impose."

"There was no imposition, Jay. I'm sorry you lost your friend."

"We'll have services as soon as possible. I'll be back at school in a few days."

"Take the time you need." Sandra looked more closely at her. Circles rimmed her eyes and her face was smudged with strain. "You look awful."

Jay's mouth twisted in a tired smile. "I'm not feeling my fashionable best."

"I'm sorry," Sandra said quickly. "I didn't mean . . . I guess, I don't think of you as fragile."

Jay lifted her coffee mug to her lips with both hands, gazing at Sandra as she sipped. "You're a soft touch, Dr. Ross. But don't worry, I won't ruin your tough reputation at school."

Avoiding Jay's smiling eyes, Sandra poured herself another cup of coffee.

Jay asked, "What are you doing on Friday, the week after Thanksgiving?"

Sandra hesitated, then remembered. "I'll be attending your family's benefit."

Jay swallowed the last of her coffee and washed her mug in the sink. "I have one more favor to ask."

"Yes?"

"Where did you put my car keys?"

Sandra set her unfinished coffee aside as Jay's car pulled away from the curb. She headed for the bathroom, undressing slowly. She stepped into the shower and closed her eyes against the spray. It wasn't fair that people died before Thanksgiving. How could anyone offer up thanks in the face of despair? And to whom did one complain? Atheism gave no comfort, religion offered faith but few answers. Humanity was left to muddle its way through.

Outside, blue water and a yellow sky betrayed her feelings. She had always relied on bare branches to fight the bitterness. Their sharp violence ripped at the sky, releasing snow to save the world from naked cold. California hid its harsh nature behind the evergreens. Now, more than ever, Sandra longed for the color of winter.

# Chapter 9

Loud, generous and informal, Amy's family welcomed Sandra for Thanksgiving happily, then left her to fend for herself. Animated argument dominated conversation. The tension of feeling an outsider faded and Sandra relaxed without its weight, not realizing until it lifted that she had shouldered the burden.

Amy guided her through a maze of guests, including Sam and Evie Kaplan.

"The Kaplans and Greenburgs have shared Thanksgiving for years," Amy explained.

Sam placed a hand on Sandra's shoulder. "You'll be at the holiday benefit, of course."

Sandra nodded an affirmative although Sam seemed to be stating fact rather than asking a question.

"Sam," Amy said with a note of impatience, "couldn't you have spared your newest faculty member some of the dirty politics, at least for one semester?"

"Nonsense. Sandra's a talented colleague."

Sandra, uncomfortable as the topic of conversation, turned to Evie. "You must have known Amy's parents for some time," she said, attempting to shift the dialogue.

"Since Amy was in high school," Evie said. "She always argues with Sam. When she stops, her father takes over. Wait and see."

Hands on her hips, Amy glared at Sam for a moment longer before her gaze softened on Evie. "Evie paints brilliantly," Amy said without warning.

"My father was a painter," Sandra said.

Evie's smile touched her. "What is his preferred medium, do you know?"

"Oil." Sandra took a breath. Why had she brought it up? "I'm sorry, it was a hobby for him, really. He's been dead for many years." She surprised herself by adding truthfully, "I'd love to see your work."

"I'll take you." Amy's statement allowed no room for argument. "We'll take the grand city tour."

The Kaplans wandered away across the living room but Amy caught Sandra by the arm.

"Stay close," Amy pleaded. "My mother hasn't scolded me in at least ten minutes."

Before Sandra could answer, Amy's father descended with a tray of hors d'oeuvres.

"Sam thinks he can talk circles around me," he complained happily. "What does he know?" He eyed Sandra sharply. "You look like an expert, come help an old man."

Amy threw up her hands in exasperation.

"Your mother is in the kitchen," her father instructed. "So, go see if she needs some help."

"Traitor," Amy accused as Sandra glanced back.

Motioning Sandra to the sofa, Mr. Greenburg set his tray of food aside. "They can serve themselves if they're hungry, right? Amy is a good student but she studies the mind. I don't know this psychology. Sam tells me you're good in history?"

"Sam likes a good argument," Sandra said with a smile.

As she suspected, no further introduction was needed. Sam leaned forward in his chair and words poured out. Conversation, Sandra thought, like history, followed a familiar course.

Patterns, according to Amy, always repeated. But Amy understood psychology. Sandra catalogued the consequences of action but remained wary of the motivations. Improvisation made the passage interesting; venturing off the usual avenues created intolerable tension.

"Harry, your guests are starving." Mrs. Greenburg's bosom rose like fresh bread under her apron. "Eat now, argue later," she admonished her husband. "Come to the table."

How many wars, Sandra wondered, could have been avoided with ample food? But the flow of thought was not easily averted. Positions were again staked out around the table, opinions carved and served with gravy through the feast.

Sandra ate sparingly. She enjoyed the conversation but the meal lacked seasoning. And her own family memories crowded her at the table.

The Kaplans drove her home. Seated in the back of their small car, Sandra's thoughts transported her to a childhood holiday. Where had they been? At her grandparents'. The Kaplans murmured together in the front seat. Sandra heard her parents' voices, but couldn't make out the words. They had been arguing, soft voices strained with tension. What were they fighting about? Her father's work.

"Painting won't feed your family." Her mother's voice raised slightly, carrying to the back seat.

It was wrong. Her father practiced law, painting only a hobby. But the easel stood empty that winter. Her father stayed away until late at night and the house remained quiet.

She remembered the starched dress she wore at the spring funeral when her grandfather died. Afterwards, she ran upstairs to change. A sound in the attic enticed her up another flight of stairs and there was her father, still in his black suit, preparing a canvas. He looked at her and winked, late afternoon sun shining through the tiny window on his face.

Sandra thanked the Kaplans and let herself into her house without turning on the light. She pulled a wine bottle from the rack, unmindful of the label. It was all good wine. Her father's taste had been excellent. She savored it slowly, thinking about family.

Organized like their mother, a lawyer by trade like their father, her brother had assumed the role of family patriarch. Brian would have Christmas on the Cape again this year, saltwater and snow.

Sandra secretly believed it must have snowed in heaven. Why else would hell be full of fire? If heaven and hell existed, Sandra thought as she waited without hope for sleep, she would never know the difference. Even the violent religion of the Middle Ages had not been able to mark one landscape from the other. Evil and honesty remained as indistinguishable as California sun in morning fog.


Even the city's fog couldn't mask the force of cultural elegance at the Hope Foundation benefit. A formal hall, decorated for the gala affair, danced with tuxedoed waiters. Champagne accompanied introductions; men and women chatted easily, entertaining one another in evening dress. Sandra's tailored wool fell just to her knees. Many of the women, she noted, sported full-length gowns and bare backs.

"Hey, sheriff." Amy handed Sandra a glass of champagne. "You just don't look ready for a showdown."

Sandra smiled at Amy's greeting. "I had to check my boots and spurs at the door."

Amy's dress, while not floor length, showed the sleek lines of custom design. Sandra didn't want to guess its price. The prestigious evening did not include a sit-down dinner, rather, an elaborate buffet dominated one side of the ballroom. The effect was informal and glamorous, designed, no doubt, to remind guests that the Hope family shared their wealth wisely. Sandra quickly abandoned champagne for mineral water, the wine from another sleepless night pulsing as a headache behind her eyes.

Several small rooms showcased the work of sponsored artists. Sandra knew that members of her department received research funding from the foundation, but talk seemed limited to art. She found the lack of proposal discussions odd, even overly polite in such company.

Sandra pulled Amy aside. "No one talks about the money."

"Noticed that, did you? Those are the rules, kid. Direct proposals are generally turned down. The foundation doesn't advertise. It invites. And don't look now but there's an invitation walking your way."

Amy grabbed a passing group and mingled herself away. Sandra recognized the approaching figure of the foundation's president and hostess, Mrs. Roberta Hope.

Roberta Hope followed an invisible red carpet across the ballroom floor. She cut a straight swath through the crowded room and a sea of guests obligingly parted. Sandra stood still, watching the procession of one move regally toward her.

"Dr. Ross, isn't it?" Mrs. Hope extended a polished hand. "I'm sorry we haven't been formally introduced. I'm Roberta Hope."

Sandra extended her hand in turn. "It's an honor to meet you, Mrs. Hope. The foundation is truly impressive."

Roberta smiled, not warmly, and took the compliment as her due. Sandra guessed Roberta Hope to be roughly ten years her senior, but the woman radiated poise and power that had nothing to do with simple seniority. Glacial, Sandra thought, and shivered inwardly at the impression.

"My daughter, Jessica, knows you."

"I supervise Jay's research project. She's an excellent student."

"I'm so glad you can appreciate her intellect. The family is pleased that she has finally committed herself to its full use."

Sandra said, "I understand that Jay owns a successful business."

Brown eyes, a shade darker than Jay's, flashed sharply. Sandra found herself looking for the humor she so often saw in Jay's expression, but none was evident.

"Your work is quite interesting." Roberta made no attempt to guide a conversation. She simply addressed the topics as she wished.

"My position with the university is fairly new," Sandra responded. "Are you referring to any research in particular?"

"You were in Boston previously, I believe? Your dissertation was well-received. You wrote on developments in medieval society, as I recall."

The statement startled Sandra. Her dissertation had certainly been well-received but it was not generally a topic of cocktail conversation. Roberta, apparently, had done some homework. Sandra smiled politely. It was her job, after all, to assign and correct homework.

She said easily, "My work described the impact of

political forces on the influence of the Christian Church in France during the first half of the fourteenth century." She paused and added, "I'm always cautioning my students against taking too broad a view."

"Indeed."

Sandra sensed movement and turned as Jay appeared. She wore a tailored masculine suit complete with silk tie and vest. The bandage on her hand, Sandra noted, was smaller.

"Jessica, dear, I was just discussing historical research with our new professor."

"I don't believe the family owns this one, Mother."

Roberta ignored her daughter's comment. She said to Sandra, "Really, Doctor, I'm sure there will be ample opportunity for you to continue with your studies here in Berkeley. The foundation is eager to review your latest proposal."

Sandra felt momentarily light-headed. The buzz of conversation muted to stillness and she watched the party swirl silently around her. The alarming sense of detachment receded; Sandra felt her perceptions shift and realign, as if an internal ice floe had thawed suddenly and with great upheaval.

Sandra realized that Roberta was regarding her closely, no doubt waiting for her to accept the bribe. Take our money, save our daughter. Except they didn't want their daughter saved, only gift-wrapped in time for the holidays.

Amy had been wrong. The Hope family didn't play with fire. They used ice to freeze the world into a never-changing image of their own making. The true danger waited in the thaw.

Sandra looked directly at Roberta Hope and said, "I'm sorry. It's time for me to leave. Good night."

Just outside the entrance, someone called her name. Sandra accepted the terms of her integrity but she simply had no energy at the moment for a battle. Unwilling to turn, she continued to walk up the long drive. Out of sight of the house, the night seemed shockingly clear. Sandra paused to catch her breath and felt a light touch on her arm.

The familiar voice said, "Sandra, I apologize."

"There's no need, Jay. There's no need to apologize."

"I think there is."

"Then walk me to the station. I'm too tired for anything else."

Sandra headed automatically for the subway but Jay caught her arm and led her to the taxi stand. Without a word, Jay helped Sandra into the cab and paid the driver. Sandra heard Jay give her address through the open window. She leaned forward.

"Thank you, Jay."

Jay said nothing, her eyes indistinct in the streetlight, copper melted into darkness. Sandra looked back as the cab pulled away but she glimpsed only gray shadows, the color of ash.

# Chapter 10

Sandra hung up the phone, completing a mental checklist of her plans to visit Boston, thinking fondly of old friends. Stretching, she considered the evening ahead. Saturday night. She could go out, take in a movie. Automatically, she moved to call Amy but stopped, her hand on the phone.

Only yesterday she had been surrounded by the academic and artistic elite. Her first impression had been of ice, but maybe Amy was right to warn of fire. Certainly ambition burned in the Hope household. How would Jay say it? The House of

Hope. They burned dreams using greed for kindling, an emotion as tinder-dry as the hills.

Sandra glanced out the window. Fire or ice. It didn't matter which one threatened, she feared them both. The last of the afternoon sun had disappeared behind clouds and the inevitable fog was on the approach. Sandra turned on a lamp and let the light push the foothills farther away. Selecting Vivaldi, she turned up the volume on her old stereo. She clattered pots and pans in the kitchen, preparing to cook, comforted by her own familiar company.

A persistent knock interrupted the strenuous grating of Parmesan. Sandra answered the door holding a dishtowel.

"Hi." Jay leaned against the jamb, casual in jeans and a loose sweater. "Smells great."

"Red sauce. Come in." Sandra left Jay to shut the door and returned to the kitchen. Jay appeared a moment later, watching as Sandra chopped parsley at a standing butcher's block.

"You're a good cook."

Sandra smiled. "Most people wait until they've tasted the food."

"Fresh Parmesan and parsley." Jay nodded her approval. "Is it a hobby or a passion?"

"Cooking? A hobby, I guess. I find it relaxing. I have friends in Boston who are definitely passionate. They taught me a few things."

Sandra uncorked a wine bottle and poured two glasses without bothering to ask Jay's preference. Jay accepted the wine and took a stool at the counter.

"Do you miss Boston?"

"Yes, I do. I'm planning to visit during winter break."

Jay smiled but her eyes didn't. She would understand Jay, Sandra thought, when she could translate the emotions in her eyes.

Jay asked, "Are you having second thoughts about the West Coast?"

Sandra put down her knife. "My second thoughts," she said, "are of my own making. Not yours, and certainly not from your family."

"I didn't think you would scare easily." The smile reached Jay's eyes before she added seriously, "I apologize again for last night."

"Again, no apology is necessary." Sandra turned resolutely toward the stove where water boiled energetically. "It seems I owe you for cab fare. Are you hungry?"

"Starved."

As Sandra put the pasta in to cook she thought about Jay's comment. She wasn't scared of Jay's family. Memories of her own family were terrifying enough. The old fear bullied her like an overgrown playmate, and the taunts grew increasingly tiresome.

Sandra prepared a salad, then stepped from the kitchen to the wide front room. The leather couch stared at the hills. Behind the couch stood a round table of yellow pine, the wood stained and polished but otherwise uncovered. Sandra set the table while Jay moved to inspect the fireplace. In a moment, she had wood stacked and placed a match to kindling. The fire snapped behind its wire screen.

Sandra carried plates of pasta and sauce to the table. She said, "The wine is in the kitchen."

Jay refilled their glasses and sat down.

"The fire's nice." Sandra served salad into bowls.

"The fog's come in." Jay sipped her wine.

"I didn't know it would be so foggy here. I'm not used to it."

"Better than snow."

"I don't mind the snow," Sandra said. "Snow covers the trees and transforms them. Fog just hides everything."

Jay held up her glass. "To transformation."

Sandra touched Jay's glass with her own. The sound of the toast lingered over the table. Sandra brought the glass to her lips and watched as Jay did the same. The fog couldn't hide everything, Sandra thought as she tasted her wine, and here was another frightening horizon.

Jay tasted her food. "Sandra, this is wonderful." Her voice held genuine enthusiasm.

"This dish was popular with the Boston crowd, too."

"Tell me about your life there."

Sandra twirled pasta on her plate. "What do you want to know?"

"Tell me about your friends."

"A group of us read books and took turns writing, mostly short fiction or essays. We met through the fall and winter but as soon as the buds came out we gave it up. We called ourselves 'Empty Trees or Empty Pages.' It was a standing joke that none of us ever wrote anything worthwhile in the spring."

Jay asked, "What is it about winter that inspires you?"

"I like the bare branches. I know some people find them depressing, skeletal, but I think they're beautiful. They're a promise, an artist's frame. Nature leaves more to the imagination in winter."

Jay had stopped eating, her fingers resting lightly

on the stem of her wineglass. "I know you're a researcher, but you sound like an artist."

Sandra smiled and resumed twirling pasta. "What's your favorite time of year?"

"I suppose, autumn," Jay said slowly. "That's when change seems the most imminent."

"More so than spring?"

"Warm weather is too subtle. Cold invigorates."

Sandra applauded. "Spoken like a true New Englander."

Awkwardness evaporated into companionship and they ate in comfortable silence. Sandra carried coffee to the couch as Jay placed another log on the grate.

Jay held her mug in both hands. "Thank you for sharing your evening with me. I appreciate your company."

Sandra watched her in the firelight — an insistent young woman willing to dig up the family foundation just to get a good look at old demons. It was a rare family that shared its secrets. The coldest households layered truth with half-truths and half-truth with lies, illusory insulation that failed, inevitably, to protect.

Jay smiled at Sandra's silence. "What are you pondering, Professor?"

"Honesty. And I keep meaning to ask how you know where I live."

"I have an unusual code of ethics," Jay said lightly. "Don't ask." She looked up. "You have a great deal of integrity. I admire that in you."

"Honesty needs more courage than integrity."

"Aren't they the same?"

"I think integrity can sometimes be a matter of following form," Sandra replied. "Honesty requires admitting to fears and flaws."

Jay curled her legs on the couch. "What are you afraid of, Sandra?"

She feared a bite that had happened long ago. She still fought the venom inside, clinging to her unchanged core like fragile shells to rocks in a tidal pool. She feared the same bite she knew her father had suffered and, if she let go, she was afraid she would be tumbled like him at the mercy of the waves, crushed by their brutal force. Even if she had the strength to swim beyond the breakers, what guarantee that deeper waters were any safer?

"I'm afraid I haven't gone far enough, that there's a path I've missed along the way," Sandra answered. "Aren't you ever afraid of getting lost?"

"I'm not lost." Jay laughed. "Just cast out. My dilemma has always been deciding whether to fight my way back into one fortress or build another."

"Is a fortress necessary?"

"How else do you protect yourself?"

Sandra couldn't answer.

After a silence Jay spoke softly, "You don't have much practice breaking rules, do you?"

"I have a hard time not thinking about consequences."

Sandra looked at Jay. The desire in the young woman's eyes was easy to read. Sandra felt an answering desire rise as heat to her face.

Sandra said earnestly, "I have to protect what I believe in, Jay. You're a student. I can justify my feelings toward you. I could never justify the action."

"It seems to me," Jay said, her voice still low, "that for someone so afraid of getting lost, you have a very good sense of direction."

"You came here, Jay."

"I like being here. I like the way your seriousness can't quite hide your concern." Jay smiled. "I'm going to keep coming here until you tell me to leave."

Sandra hesitated. She could face her fear but she could not speak it, and without fear, courage didn't matter. All she had left was honesty. It was the best she could do, then, to be honest.

"I don't want you to leave."

Jay leaned over and Sandra accepted the embrace. She wasn't lost, but her landscape had changed. Touching Jay's face, tasting her lips, she felt she couldn't bear to miss the beauty.

A remnant of doubt wrapped itself in her thoughts, damping the warmth that seeped under her breastbone. Sandra pulled back.

"I'm sorry. I never meant to let this happen. It can't happen."

"Nothing's happened," Jay responded. "Not yet."

"It can't, Jay. Surely you know that I have a responsibility as a teacher. I could never permit such an abuse of my authority."

Jay laughed. "Abuse? I don't feel abused in the least. Sandra, please, give me a little credit. Authority is not an issue here."

"I have a responsibility," Sandra repeated.

"What happened to honesty?"

Sandra stared at Jay. How had she come to the edge of this decision so quickly? Was she prepared to throw away her trust in academics, to risk damaging her own values, her career? Had Jay not asked for honesty, Sandra would have lied. She would have confessed to flattery, apologized for flirtation and said good night. But she had been trying to sleep with half-truths for years. Suddenly she craved a night without deception.

Sandra shook her head at her own arguments. She said lightly, "Don't you think I'm a little old for you, Jay? I'm closer in age to your mother than to you."

Jay rested an arm along the back of the couch. Her tone held amusement as she answered, "I've never considered age to be a barrier to beauty. And I've never, ever been attracted to my mother."

Sandra flushed. "I didn't mean to imply — "

"It's your softness," Jay interrupted. "Underneath that tenacious, academic exterior, there's . . . tenderness." The humor had vanished from her voice. "I don't know why you hide it."

Sandra reached to touch Jay's hair, letting the soft thickness cover her fingers. "You're very beautiful, Jay."

"Not too young?"

"Brash, impatient, intelligent." She paused, knowing it wasn't just the intelligence in Jay's eyes that compelled desire. A sliver of pain slipped in behind the laughter and touched her own sharp need. She wanted to soothe them both. She took Jay's hand. A bandage still covered the cut from the broken bottle. "Are you healing?"

"Yes."

"Come to bed."

In Sandra's bedroom, they undressed each other, kissing. Fear flared again and Sandra caught her breath, holding Jay's face with both hands.

Jay rested her palms on Sandra's hips. "Have you ever made love with a woman?"

Surprised by the question, Sandra said, "Yes, of course. Do I seem so naive?"

"Scared." Jay smiled.

Sandra closed her eyes. Sex didn't scare her, just the risk of self-exposure. She had the feeling that she was venturing onto the narrowest of ledges.

"Underneath the surface," Jay whispered, "love is very soft, very simple."

Sandra placed her hands firmly on Jay's back, pulling her down to the bed, seeking the strength of Jay's body on top of her own. Then she rolled to put Jay beneath her, defying the edge and damning the distance over which she searched for an answer. Love, for her, was neither hard nor soft, not difficult or simple. It was, at the moment, the only place to stand.

Later that night as they lay warmly together, Sandra glimpsed a thin band of sky defying the mist. The fog had retreated, leaving delicate moonlight to trace a shifting snowflake pattern on the skin of the woman beside her.

Sandra opened her eyes to cold sunlight, the empty bed beside her still warm. In her mind she heard whispers of concern, stirrings of complications. Closing her eyes, she thought only of her own breathing. Then slowly and with great care she blanked her mind and remembered with her body. She relaxed again into the soft swell of emotion, listening to the sound of running water. The taps were shut off and a short while later she felt Jay bending close. She opened her eyes but said nothing.

Jay whispered, "Good morning." A pause and then, "Are you okay?"

Jay was dressed, sitting beside her on the bed.

"Yes." Sandra lifted a hand to smooth her palm across Jay's cheek.

Jay's lips were a brief caress. "I have to work. I'll call you later."

Sandra heard the door close and fell back into dreamless sleep. When she opened her eyes again the day had warmed to mid-morning. She showered and dressed. An hour later, the coffee pot was empty and Sandra couldn't remember reading a word, although the Sunday paper lay in disarray before her.

Refusing to let herself think, she turned to housework, vacuuming, dusting, scrubbing. She was contemplating polishing the windows when she gave it up. Catching a late afternoon bus, she headed across town.

Houses over the bay clung crablike to the hillside. Thinking of earthquakes, she recalled pictures of crumpled houses, accordioned roads. Looking up now at the precarious beauty, she wondered if the city knew what it was doing after all.

Sandra entered Jay's store and edged her way to the back, pretending interest in a wall tapestry. Jay's attention remained focused on a complaining customer. Sandra tried to listen unobtrusively.

"I'm not looking for a period piece. This is for my study at home. I want something with character, something unique."

The customer looked to be in his forties, casually

dressed in jeans and western boots. He sported a
well-trimmed beard and long hair in the style of an
affluent hippie.

He continued impatiently, "Kozy said Jonathan
has a showroom."

Jay said something in a low voice which Sandra
could not hear. The customer listened intently.

"Expensive," was his curt response.

Jay pulled a card from the breast pocket of her
blouse and wrote on it briefly. "I'll ask Jonathan to
arrange for you to see a few pieces."

She handed the card to the customer and shook
his hand, watching until the door closed behind him.
Smiling, she turned toward Sandra.

"You can come out of hiding." She said as Sandra
stepped from behind a potted fern, "I'll be closing in
about an hour. Can I meet you somewhere?"

"Do you want coffee? I'll get us something down
the street."

Jay didn't hesitate. "Double espresso, as is."

Sandra was back soon holding covered paper cups.
Jay opened the door behind the counter and Sandra
had a chance to study the small storage room. All
signs of broken glass and other disarray were gone.
Shelves stacked with catalogues and boxed files lined
the walls. The old leather armchair, soft and patched,
claimed one corner under a standing lamp. The worn
Oriental rug covering the cement floor looked freshly
vacuumed. A space heater purred. Jay asked, "Will
you be comfortable in here?"

"Yes. How's Jonathan?"

"He's doing as well as can be expected."

Sandra's gaze dropped to the bandage on Jay's
hand. She stared at the gauze, suddenly awkward.

Jay picked up one of Sandra's hands and brought it to her lips.

"Go mind the store." Sandra reclaimed her hand and sketched a wave to Jay. "Take your time. I'll wait." She turned to inspect the contents of a bookcase.

Jay shut the door softly, leaving Sandra alone.

The bookcase held volumes on furniture design and art history and an eclectic selection of historical works. Early American dates were well-represented and Sandra guessed that those periods were favored by customers. A volume on ancient weaponry contained penciled notes; page markers peeked out of several similar books. Sandra noted that Jay's poetry books also filled a shelf. Eventually, she pulled her own book from her shoulder bag and settled into the armchair, comfortable in the warmth of Jay's office.

A tap at the door sounded as Jay stepped into the room. Behind her, blinds had been drawn across the shop windows, the front lights turned out. Sandra sat curled in the old armchair. She let her book fall shut in her lap as Jay pulled up a chair and straddled it backwards.

Jay's tone was matter-of-fact. "I'll be withdrawing my research project first thing in the morning."

Sandra kept her own voice calm. "You'll do no such thing." She took a breath and halted, suddenly at a loss.

"I want you more than I need academic acceptance," Jay said impatiently.

Sandra found her words again. "Are your goals so easily averted?"

"I have no goals."

Sandra waited. She couldn't tell if Jay meant to be serious or sarcastic.

When she continued, Jay sounded tired. "I've been fighting my family for a long time, Sandra. And I was just starting to think it might be easier to do it their way. Then I met you."

"If you don't want to go to school," Sandra replied evenly, "that's your decision. But I won't give you an excuse. Figure out what you want, Jay, for yourself."

"I want you."

Sandra uncurled herself from the armchair. She had been honest before, she thought, and it may have been a mistake, but she could afford nothing less than honesty now.

"Jay," Sandra said carefully, "I care about you, and I want to be with you, to enjoy your companionship and... more. But you came to me first because I'm a teacher. I can see now that I will fail us both if I allow this to continue. I'm sorry."

Jay was slow to answer. "What are you protecting, my academic standing or your own security?"

Sandra stood, placing her book back into her bag, collecting her jacket. She said quietly, "Both."

# Chapter 11

Sandra passed the week alternating between fevered concentration and distraction. Amy called to insist on a date to San Francisco and Sandra readily agreed, eager for any outlet.

They drove into the city.

Holiday shoppers jammed the streets and competed for parking. Amy maneuvered steep hills expertly and Sandra renewed her own faith in the wisdom of public transit. They wandered through gift shops and art galleries, Amy shopping extravagantly. Sandra selected presents that could be packed into her suitcase. At dinner they discussed paintings over steamed crab and sourdough bread.

Amy asked, "What did your father paint?"

"Seascapes, mostly. He was an amateur."

"You don't talk about your family."

"My father killed himself when I was seventeen."

"What happened?"

"No one talked about it and I left for college. He was sort of the family failure."

"And you've had a compulsion for lost causes ever since, hmm?"

"Does anyone ever tell you to keep your devastating insights to yourself?"

"All the time," Amy said with a smile.

"What do the paintings mean to you?"

Amy shrugged. "I don't understand art at all."

Laughing, Sandra asked, "Why did you choose psychology?"

"You've seen my family. I figured I could understand them or kill them. I loathe the thought of prison."

"And do you understand them now?"

"Yes, of course. But it doesn't seem to help."

"Amy, does anyone get along with their family?"

"Some people accept their families, others accept themselves in spite of their families. I charge a lot for this, dear. What's on your mind?"

"Sorry." Sandra frowned. "I'm visiting my brother for Christmas, that's all."

"Why did you decide to move to Berkeley?"

Sandra looked up in surprise. "Is a good job offer a good reason?"

"For some people. Is it a good reason for you?"

"Actually, it surprised the hell out of me that I

received an offer so quickly." Sandra reached for a piece of bread. "I thought it was time for a change of scenery, okay?"

"The problem with internal scenery," Amy commented, "is that it travels with you. You can buy a new roadmap but you still have to cross the same terrain."

"I like my job and you're fired."

"Hit a nerve, hmm?"

"You're impossible."

"According to my father," Amy easily changed tack, "Sam Kaplan thinks very highly of you."

"To tell you the truth, that part surprises me, too. I know I'm good at what I do, but why would Sam go out of his way to recruit me?"

"Why not you?"

"Because Sam plays politics. Everyone does, you said so yourself. Even his wife admitted to me that Sam compromises when he has to. I can't understand why in this case he didn't make a more political appointment."

Amy remained thoughtful for a moment, then asked, "Are you sure you're not a political appointment? Sam can't ignore the status he gains by having Jay Hope's supervisor in his department."

"Sam seemed as surprised as everyone else when Jay asked me to supervise her project. Besides, he couldn't have known about it in advance." Sandra frowned. "If Sam wants status, why didn't he hire someone with more experience? It just doesn't make sense."

"Well it's lucky for him you're such a good supervisor."

Amy smiled but Sandra felt the words like a slap

in the face. Possibly, she told herself harshly, if she kept her priorities in line and focused on the job she was paid to do, then just possibly she might salvage this supervision.

Amy tapped a polished fingernail on the table in front of Sandra. "Don't look so glum. Ask me for a date and I'll show you the women's bars."

Sandra shook her head. "Sorry. Shopping exhausts me."

"That's pathetic," Amy said unsympathetically. "I won't press, but only because it's your first semester. As soon as finals are over, I'm going to fix you up."

Amy excused herself, heading for the ladies' room. Sandra sighed. Finals were the last thing on her mind.

Sandra's notes and comments filled the margins on the first draft of Jay's paper. The pages before her had arrived by mail with a return envelope enclosed. Jay, apparently, did not intend to make a personal appearance. The research revealed technical excellence. Sandra had come to expect no less. But the writing was withered, flat and lifeless, as if Jay had already lost interest.

Was it simply the absence of Jay's company, Sandra wondered, or had Jay withdrawn her intellect as well as her presence? Sandra frowned at the pages in frustration. Perhaps she had no right to emotion outside of the classroom, but she could damn well insist on it academically. Dull was something she would never tolerate from Jay.

Sandra stood and paced to the window where her

gaze met an annoying tangle of leaves. Ignoring the return envelope, she placed Jay's work in a clean folder and piled it with her class notes. She had a seminar to give. Then she would see about Jay.

The sun had already set as Sandra walked up the north-side hill. Late customers and light from the closing shops spilled onto the streets. Jay stood motionless in the storefront as Sandra approached. Whether or not she was visible to Jay on the darkened street, Sandra couldn't tell.

Jay looked toward the door as Sandra pushed it open. "Hello, Sandra. I'll be closing in just a few minutes."

"I'll wait."

Jay made no move to open the back office. Sandra sat in one of the modern chairs placed for customers by the counter. She selected a notebook from her shoulder bag and began to review lecture notes. Jay stood at the window a moment longer and then quietly and efficiently closed shop. Sandra looked up as the front light was shut off. Jay turned the closed sign on the door.

Jay said, "I'm famished. Let's get something to eat."

"No. I came to make sure you looked at my notes on your draft, that's all."

Jay crossed her arms. "I refuse to be educated on an empty stomach."

Sandra meant to protest but Jay was heading out the back entrance. Sandra followed her into the alley.

"Sandra," Jay said in a subdued voice, "you could have mailed the damn paper. But since you're standing here in the cold, tell me all about it over hot food."

Sandra sighed. Jay was right, she had no business being here. This was no academic errand of mercy; she was indulging herself in an unprofessional vanity. She just wanted to be sure that Jay heard what she had to say. Jay held open the door to the car and Sandra got in, suddenly hungry.

As they drove west and then south, Sandra recognized landmarks in her own neighborhood. The restaurant was less than half a dozen blocks from her house. She stuck close to Jay in the press of bodies. Warm and clearly well-fed, patrons overflowed the chairs and tables. A waitress greeted Jay by name and quickly seated them to one side, away from the crowd. As the waitress departed, another woman approached their table.

"Jay, it's good to see you again." She was about Sandra's age, with dark gray hair pulled back at her neck.

Jay made introductions. "Sandra, I'd like you to meet Kozy Hirota, the owner. Kozy, Sandra Ross teaches at the university."

Kozy kissed Jay's cheek and extended a hand to Sandra. "I'm delighted to meet you. Jay mentioned she had a new friend at school."

Not entirely accurate, Sandra mused, but it was not a point she cared to argue.

Jay said to Kozy, "I found a piece you might like. I'll bring it over if you're interested."

"Come by the house for a real dinner," she suggested. "In the meantime, I'll see if we can find you something decent to eat around here." She smiled at Sandra, asking, "Have you any dietary restrictions? Allergies?"

Intrigued, Sandra shook her head no.

Kozy disappeared in the direction of the kitchen, greeting other customers on her way.

"She's an incredible chef," Jay said. "Unfortunately, she doesn't have a chance to do much cooking anymore."

Curious, Sandra asked, "How did you meet?"

"Jonathan introduced us. She collects Japanese porcelain, vases mostly, and some pottery."

"That sounds beautiful. I haven't seen anything like that in your shop."

"A lot of trade takes place at auctions. Jonathan has innumerable contacts and I try to keep an eye out for special requests."

The waitress returned with bowls of steaming miso soup.

"I'm never allowed to order," Jay said. "I hope you'll be happy with Kozy's choice of menu."

Sandra tasted the rich broth and began to relax.

"Delicious," she murmured, the strain of the day fading a little.

She hadn't realized the extent of her fatigue. Jay also seemed to be relaxing, chatting easily.

"Kozy's family emigrated from Japan to Hawaii. She came to Berkeley to study hotel management but dropped out and convinced her family to finance her restaurant instead of her education."

"A generous family," Sandra remarked.

"She's a generous woman. She helped her brother buy into a hotel in San Francisco. A successful venture, I believe."

The waitress returned and the table was filled with dishes of food. Jay identified raw tuna rolled in seaweed presented with ginger and horseradish. Chicken in a mild, curried sauce was served in bowls over thick noodles. Crisp, steamed vegetables tasted of sesame.

"Jay, this is exquisite. I had no idea this restaurant was here." Sandra delighted in the taste and texture of the unfamiliar food, sampling tentatively at first and then eating with enjoyment.

"A favorite among the locals," Jay replied, indicating the crowded tables nearby. "I was in Boston a few years back when I worked for the auctions. We had a terrific Indian meal."

"Central Square, probably. You'd love the North End." Sandra allowed herself a moment of nostalgia before pushing the plates and memories aside. She pulled out the folder with Jay's work. "Let's go over the paper."

Jay handled the shift neutrally. "How did you find my draft?"

"Technically excellent."

"And?"

"It's flat, Jay. I don't know how else to say it. The excitement you generated in your initial research is missing. You don't convey your data with conviction."

Jay leaned into the table on folded arms. "You want a lot, don't you, Professor."

Sandra said steadily, "I want your best, Jay. You can do better." She closed the folder and placed it on the table. "My notes are here as well."

Jay considered the folder but made no move to pick it up. "You have a lot of nerve," she said quietly, "asking for my best when you've settled for mediocre."

The comfortable noise of the restaurant faded into the background. Sandra was aware only of the

111

woman seated across from her, and her heart sounded a rhythm like surf on sand.

"Is my life so simple to understand that you can judge my choices?" Sandra asked softly.

"You're willing to ask for passion from others. What about you? What makes you passionate, Sandra?"

She wanted to tell Jay that she had no right to ask, but she certainly asked the same thing of herself, night after night, and the questions kept her awake, refusing to let her sleep because she refused to answer.

Sandra flinched, startled by the sound of a dish dropping in the kitchen. Jay waited quietly for an answer that Sandra still could not speak. Bowls were cleared away and Kozy returned to their table. She and Jay spoke for a few moments but Sandra made no effort to follow the conversation.

Kozy turned to Sandra. "Was the food satisfactory?"

Sandra tried to express appreciation. "The food was wonderful. Thank you."

Kozy smiled. "Please have Jay bring you again soon."

Sandra reached for her pocketbook but stopped as Jay shook her head slightly.

"Thanks, Kozy." Jay stood and kissed the older woman's cheek. "I'll give you a call."

On the street, Sandra turned to Jay. "Am I wrong or did we forgo a monetary exchange?"

Jay laughed. "I don't take a commission when I work for her. Things even out in the end."

"Thank you, Jay. Perhaps I should buy furniture from you, too."

Jay started to say something but bit off her words. "I'll drive you home."

"I can walk. It's close."

"The Dodge is closer. Come on."

A few minutes later, Jay pulled the car to a stop in front of Sandra's house.

"I'm flying to San Diego this weekend to evaluate an estate. Would you like to come?"

"Jay, please," Sandra began a protest.

Jay said forcefully, "Do we have to stop being friends? I don't want to pretend that I don't enjoy your company. Let's get out of here for the weekend. You work too hard."

"You're impulsive."

"I'm rich, too." Jay winked. "But I don't suppose you'd let me buy your plane ticket?"

"Let me think about it," Sandra said.

"You'll find a reason to say no."

"Probably."

"Come with me."

Sandra chastised herself for being drawn into the conversation. Caution or passion, she told herself, take your pick. She wanted to run from the insistence of risk until she reached solid ground, but she had been climbing to find that pointless plateau for years. There were no safe views, no rewarding vistas. Better to jump and see what she could in the fall.

Jay's arm stretched along the back of the seat, the bandage gone from her hand.

"All right," Sandra said. "I'll buy my own ticket."
She looked at Jay across the length of the car seat. Friendship, she knew, would never satisfy.

# Chapter 12

They caught a commuter flight on Friday afternoon. Circling San Diego, Sandra marveled at the city. Swimming pools seemed as common as potted plants. Lawns persisted in spite of drought, contrasting with the area's natural canyon scrub. The flight lasted just over an hour.

Sandra squinted at palm trees through the windshield of the rental car. "It's warm here."

Jay, her eyes already shaded by sunglasses, pointed out landmarks as she drove. "The earliest

California mission is here. You might find Old Town fun to explore, too."

"I'm afraid I don't know much about California's history," Sandra admitted. "You seem to know the city quite well."

"I lived here when I was twenty-three, arrogant, between jobs and out of school."

"What did you do?"

"I had affairs. Does that bother you?"

"Of course not. Unless you weren't safe. Should I be worried?"

"No." Jay looked at Sandra. "Jon's lover, Michael, rescued me from carelessness. Please don't worry."

Jay turned the car onto a crowded boulevard. "This is Hillcrest, one of the older neighborhoods. We're near the park."

"The one I saw from the air?"

"Balboa Park." Jay nodded. "I'll take you if we have time. It's lovely." Jay stopped before a gracious old hotel. "I fell in love with this place when I first saw it."

They relinquished the car to valet parking and Sandra, feeling adventurous, followed Jay inside. Stucco seemed to be the preferred style, covering the hotel and much of the surrounding architecture. A bubbling fountain in the lobby reflected wet tile.

"It's like a different world." Sandra spoke in a hushed voice, their footsteps muted by brick.

Jay inclined her head toward Sandra and said quietly, "I booked two rooms. If you'd like to save the expense, I promise to be merely a friendly and informative tour guide. Besides," her eyes smiled, "you know I don't snore."

Sandra acquiesced on practical grounds. "Thank you."

"Watch the cactus," Jay warned as they stepped off the elevator.

Rather than a hallway, the doors opened onto a small indoor patio. Brick steps descended to a veranda overlooking the street. Tables under sheltering umbrellas offered a view of treetops. Potted cactus decorated the balcony. A few guests sipped drinks on the porch.

Jay said, "The patio's better than room service."

A single corridor led to the guest rooms. Jay handed a key to Sandra as she unlocked the spacious suite.

"Make yourself comfortable."

"This is perfectly luxurious!"

The suite included a sitting room complete with couch, chairs and television. A sliding door opened onto a tiny private balcony. The bedroom featured two queen-sized beds.

"No cactus?" Sandra teased.

"Can't have the guests impaling themselves." Jay grinned.

"Jay, this is beautiful. Really."

"Can you wait to unpack? I seem to be in a permanent state of starvation."

"By all means."

The streets were bustling as daylight faded.

"It's still balmy," Sandra mused as they strolled.

"The beaches are even better. Something about the warm gulf currents. Do you swim?"

"I used to." Sandra paused. "It's been a long time."

Jay recommended a Greek restaurant close to the hotel. They ordered a selection of salads, meat and vegetable pastries, and dined in leisure. Sandra found herself yawning over coffee.

"Don't argue about who pays," Jay said as she put a credit card on the table.

"Of course I'll argue." Sandra smiled. "Tomorrow."

"I have business tomorrow afternoon," Jay said as they walked back to the hotel. "There's a couple of great bookstores around here." She looked at Sandra. "Let me know when I become a tiresome tour guide."

"Just keep us clear of the cactus."

They returned to the hotel, sharing a silence that lasted while they prepared for bed.

"You knew there were two beds," Sandra commented as she turned out the light.

"Yes. Are you comfortable?"

"The bed is fine." Sandra paused. "No, not entirely comfortable. Are you?"

"Slightly better than cactus."

"You seem to move through the world with ease," Sandra said, listening to Jay turn in the darkness.

"Practice and pretense. Were you always so cautious?"

"I suppose. Maybe not so much when I was a child."

"Were you a happy child?"

Sandra rearranged pillows, trying to find a spot of comfort.

"I thought so, until I realized my parents were unhappy."

"What are they like?"

"My parents? They're both gone now. My mother loved my father a great deal but it wasn't enough."

"Enough?" Jay's voice was soft.

"To help him find his own convictions."

"What did he do?"

"He practiced law but, to use your words, it was a pretense. He was an artist by nature. What's your pretense, Jay?"

"I lack courage."

Sandra protested gently, "You've forged your own way in spite of your family. Surely that counts as courage."

"If I'm not careful," Jay remarked, "you'll have me making confessions in my sleep. Good night, Sandra."

Sandra fell asleep, wondering why she didn't need wine, wondering if she would ever make her own confessions.

"Do people out here ever get tired of the sun?"

Sandra stood at the bedroom window brushing her hair. She gathered the fine gray strands loosely at the nape of her neck and knotted a scarf across her shoulders. Jay emerged from the bathroom buttoning a blouse, her own hair damp from the shower.

"They drink sunshine like water. Skin cancer's a bit of a problem." Jay pulled on tailored linen pants and picked up a matching jacket. "How about coffee on the patio?"

The veranda was even more beautiful by day. Brick and tile held the morning's warmth and the umbrellas remained folded in deference to December sun.

"Unbelievable," Sandra murmured.

Jay smiled. "It's nice to share the view."

Jay left by mid-morning and Sandra set off to explore the neighborhood. She quickly discovered the bookstores and browsed happily. Tour books full of photographs described the city's history and points of interest. She wandered through the art selections, wondering what books might capture Jay's imagination.

A poster for a local theater company caught her eye, advertising tickets for a play called *A Carpenter in China*.

"That's a great show." The store clerk, a young man sporting several earrings, spoke from behind the counter. "Are you new to the neighborhood?"

"Just visiting for the weekend."

"The theater's in the park and the play is fabulous. Don't miss it."

Sandra found his enthusiasm contagious. "Do you sell tickets?"

"Of course. There are still good seats left for tonight."

Sandra splurged on the best seats available and headed back to the hotel. She had plenty of time to catch up on classwork.

Jay returned just before dark.

"How'd it go?" Sandra peered over the edge of her reading glasses.

Jay stretched and her back popped loudly. "If I never inspect the legs on another table my body might forgive me," she complained. "Find anything this afternoon?"

"Theater tickets. We'll have time for dinner if we hurry."

Jay grinned. "And I was afraid you'd get lost."

"Can you get us to the park by eight?"

"Let's go."

At the theater in the round, seats filled up quickly. The play told the story of an unhappy English carpenter. He journeyed to Asia and, inspired by the new culture, crafted elaborate sculpture that he couldn't sell. When he contracted malaria and died, his family shipped the sculpture home with his body. In England, his art proved to be popular, gaining him the acceptance in death that he had craved in life.

During intermission crowds pressed outside for steaming cups of cider, tea and cocoa. Posted advertisements offered season tickets to the summer Shakespeare festival. Eucalyptus trees framed the sky and Sandra breathed the oily incense. Theater-goers exhaled quiet chants of conversation. Carillon bells chimed majestically across the park.

Jay bought cups of cocoa and Sandra smiled at the chocolaty aroma. It was not a taste she associated with theater. They spoke little. Jay seemed lost in her own thoughts, and Sandra let herself enjoy the scenery.

The roar of applause at the play's end dispelled the silent magic. The crowds once again burst forth and conversation returned to normal volume. Jay drove the few blocks back to Hillcrest, stopping at a café already filling with familiar faces from the audience.

"God, that was sad," Jay said. "A sad, beautiful story."

They shared wine and cheese, more elegant than cocoa, Sandra thought as they ordered, and also more ordinary.

"What was the saddest part for you?" Sandra asked.

Jay thought for a while. "I guess, that he never knew what joy his art could give."

"Would it have been possible for his work to be appreciated while he was still alive?"

"I doubt that it would have been so valued," Jay said seriously. "What part did you like?"

"I was glad he found fulfillment. When he was able to create, he was happy. In that moment I don't think anything else mattered to him."

"It's true," Jay said. "That was the beautiful part."

Sandra looked into Jay's warm eyes and saw the familiar pain. "What hurts you, Jay?"

Jay blinked and her eyes cleared. "It's hard to imagine creating something so personal and then handing it over to the world. I don't know if I could risk such exposure. Have you ever felt so exposed?"

"Yes. Once."

"What did you do?" Jay's eyes were earnest.

Sandra looked up, still unable to measure the depth of danger. "I tried to kill myself."

Jay leaned forward. "Tell me."

A large group made a noisy entrance, jostling their table.

Jay stood quickly. "Not here, not now. Come on."

Sandra shivered as they walked outside; the air had turned chill. They drove in silence to the hotel.

Upstairs, Sandra turned to Jay. "Tomorrow. We'll talk tomorrow."

Jay turned down her bed as Sandra stood quietly at the window. Jay moved to her, asking, "Do you need anything?"

"Just a shower."

"Extra towels are behind the door."

Sandra soaked in the hot jets of water, then dried herself and rubbed her skin vigorously with lotion. Turning off the bathroom light, she opened the door, letting her eyes adjust to the bedroom's darkness. She heard Jay turn in bed and waited for the sounds to stop. As she pulled back her own covers and lay down, the rustling from the other bed resumed and Jay sat up.

Sandra said softly, "I hope I didn't wake you."

"You didn't."

Jay crossed the distance between the beds and sat beside Sandra. Weight shifted and the covers lifted as Sandra moved to one side. She felt Jay's warmth along her body and then Jay pulled the covers close around them both.

"I'll just hold you," Jay whispered.

"I wanted to buy you a book today. I don't know what kind of art you like."

Jay wrapped her arms around Sandra. "I'll show you," she promised.



"I'll bet it's raining in San Francisco." Sandra stood in sunlight pouring through the window.

Jay blinked at the brightness, stretching in bed. "How did you sleep?"

Sandra crossed to the bed and leaned toward Jay, kissing her lightly on the forehead. "I slept little, but thank you."

Jay rubbed her eyes and yawned loudly. "What's your pleasure today, ma'am?"

"I want to see the mission and the park and anything else in between."

"The beach?"

"No." Sandra shook her head. "Not the beach."

The mission rose on a hill over an impossibly green valley. Palm trees competed with cactus for postcard photographs. Not even the noise of the freeway and the memory of shopping plazas below detracted from the mission's stately beauty.

Square, rust-colored tiles worn to grooves bordered pristine white adobe. A five-bell campanario presided over the arched entrance. Sandra tried to imagine the mission standing alone in a wilderness, a fountain of faith between desert sand and ocean salt. Unfamiliar trees bordered the churchyard and Sandra reached to touch the feathery leaves.

"Pepper trees." Jay spoke from behind her shoulder. "After a rain the air smells like a spice mill."

Blooming hibiscus surrounded the monastery ruins. Sandra wandered into the remains of old living quarters but the wood smelled musty and she returned to the courtyard, to the sound of a bubbling fountain.

Jay inspected a map detailing the progress of religion along the coast. Pious padres had formed a frail link across a region whose hell proved to be a faultline not far beneath the surface. California's native Americans had fought the cross at swordpoint and burned the first mission to the ground. Padres rebuilt; native tribes succumbed to violent conversion, their population decimated. The Christians won martyrs in the process.

Sandra was studying a statue of a man in robes.

"Not a life I find appealing," Jay remarked.

"It was such a short time ago," Sandra mused. "Our lives are very similar."

"They committed atrocities," Jay said vehemently.

"As do we all, each day, every day."

They passed through a dimly lit sanctuary into a tiny garden. More flowers banked a wishing well. The bell tower offered graceful shade from the modern world. Jay selected a bench along the tiled walkway and Sandra joined her.

Jay asked, "Do you really believe we've made such little moral progress through history?"

Sandra considered the cross perched like a lonely bird above the bells. "The roots of this country are buried in faith, but there's not enough light and air for individuality."

Jay regarded Sandra. "Do you have faith in anything in particular?"

"I thought I believed in education."

"Can you convert me?"

"No. When I reached for knowledge I bit the wrong piece of fruit."

"So, what's your sin?"

Sandra looked at Jay. "There's no serpent, you know. It's an insect."

"Are you telling me that Eve was stung by a mosquito?"

Sandra laughed. "Yes. To accept another's thoughts but ignore your own is like drinking poison."

Jay asked soberly, "What if you can't tell the difference between your own thoughts and those of everyone else?"

"I think that happens to a lot of people. We listen so long and so hard to other voices that we lose our own voice, our own thoughts."

"Is that what you teach?" Jay murmured, "Can you teach students to listen to themselves?"

"No." Sandra took a deep breath and folded her arms. "History is full of the pitfalls of people trying to learn right and wrong, trying to separate good from evil. We can learn, through experience, what works or doesn't, but each of us must uncover and embrace our own truth."

"And if we can't?" Jay persisted.

"Then we live with the pain and do our best to distract ourselves."

Jay squinted into the sun. "Sandra, are you in the wrong profession?"

"Education can be as rigid as religion. Knowledge is supposed to enlighten, but good grades aren't proof of salvation."

"What kind of proof do you need?"

"For salvation? The seasons. Which is why it makes me furious that the leaves out here won't change color."

"Sometimes I find it helpful to invent new colors." Jay added with a smile, "I've been known to lose sleep, but usually over people, not seasons."

When Sandra didn't respond, she said, "Do you often have trouble sleeping at night?"

"I rarely sleep well. It amazes me that anyone in this state can relax. You all act like you're living in heaven, knowing that at any moment the earth will open and swallow you into hell. Who could sleep? Come on, let's get lunch."

Jay insisted on mountains of guacamole. Sandra's eyes watered from peppers and onions.

"I used to order avocadoes by the case," Jay said, licking her fingers.

"What do you do with a case of avocadoes?"

"Mash them, slice them, eat them whole with pepper. Dip them in lime and drink them with beer. My faith in the divine rests with avocadoes and pomegranates."

Sandra laughed. "Is there a possible explanation for such passion?"

"Color and texture," Jay said seriously. "The world at its most beautiful is defined by color and texture. And we do have seasons in California."

"I don't see it."

"Water and fire."

Sandra leaned her elbows on the table. "You're right, of course. I thought fire paired with ice, but water at least offers the promise of life."

Jay sipped from a bottle of beer. "What do you see in history that brings you such enjoyment?"

Sandra grinned. "Color and texture?"

Jay's eyes were bright copper discs reflecting liquid sun when she laughed.

* * * * *

"'Balboa Park covers more than a thousand acres,'" Jay read from her guide book. She looked up. "That includes the zoo and a few museums."

They strolled at leisure through the botanical gardens. Sandra ran her hand along lush ferns, appreciating the dramatic beauty of birds-of-paradise. Jay led the way around a shallow pond filled with enormous lily pads. Pennies at the bottom had no doubt bought a fortune in wishes.

Sandra sat on a bench. "I didn't mean to shock you yesterday."

Jay sat beside her. "When did it happen?"

"I was still married. I knew I was unhappy. I saw a therapist for a while."

Jay stretched her legs, listening.

"All the textbooks started to sound the same," Sandra continued. "And then I went to work one day and I realized they were wrong."

"Wrong?" Jay turned slightly on the bench, looking at her.

Sandra stared into the pond as if she could find deeper meaning in the shallow water.

"They all described just one way of looking at the world." She shrugged. "I knew there must be more. I called a divorce lawyer and applied to graduate school. I had my first affair with a woman. I still felt like I was missing something. By the end of my first year in graduate school I was terrified." She glanced at Jay. "I've always relied on structure to keep track of my life. I felt like I had backed myself onto a narrow path, and I was too frightened to venture off course." Sandra sighed. "I realized all the rules had changed, but I didn't think I had the strength to define my own. I knew I couldn't live without rules."

"What did you do?"

"I went to the library. I'm always thorough with my research. I bought some pills."

Jay asked softly, "Did you take them?"

"I was going to. Then one of my professors called. He had to leave town and needed some research right away and asked if I could help. Inconvenient as it was, I didn't want to elaborate on my alternative plans."

A breeze gusted and Sandra watched eucalyptus leaves shower to the ground.

"I guess I wasn't ready to admit that I'd given up. I got his notes and spent two days in the library. I discovered an error in his premise. I couldn't believe it at first — he'd written a textbook. In fact, I edited part of it. But the more I researched his notes, the more I could see the flaw in his argument. I wrote a paper and tore him apart."

Jay chuckled. "Was he angry?"

"He wanted to co-author the paper and then he asked to supervise my dissertation."

"And the pills?"

"Success is powerful medicine. I flushed the pills, but I still think I'll drown in fear sometimes."

"Why is it you don't like the beach?"

Sandra turned away from the pond to look at Jay. "You have an inquisitive mind, don't you? Surely I've uncovered enough old memories for one day."

Jay wrapped an arm around Sandra's shoulders and with her free hand she dug a coin out of her pocket and tossed it into the pond.

Sandra smiled. "What did you wish for?"

Jay kissed Sandra's cheek. "If I tell then it won't come true."

# Chapter 13

On Monday morning they caught the first flight out of San Diego. Sandra arrived at her campus office by nine and quickly tackled the pile of papers on her desk. She was on her way to a faculty meeting when the phone rang.

"So, what's new?"

"It'll have to wait," she told Amy. "I'm in a rush."

"You didn't seem to be available over the weekend, dear."

"I was in San Diego."

"Do tell."

"Later."

Amy sighed dramatically. "I'm tied up myself all day. I'll call you tomorrow."

Sandra made a dash for the door.

After the meeting, she headed directly back to her office. If she worked through lunch she'd be set for her afternoon lecture. An hour later, the door to her office burst open and Sandra looked up, startled by the unexpected intrusion.

Roberta Hope stepped purposefully into the room and shut the door. She said abruptly, "I suggest we talk."

Sandra didn't put down her pencil. "Mrs. Hope, I have a class in fifteen minutes. Perhaps we can make a mutually convenient appointment."

Roberta sat stiffly on the edge of a chair. In her mind, Sandra saw Jay leaning back, casually attentive.

"What I have to say is brief."

Sandra waited, her pencil still poised over lecture notes.

"It has come to my attention that you have been socializing with my daughter. I ask that it stop."

Sandra said mildly, "Mrs. Hope, why do you feel it's necessary to make such a request?"

Roberta seemed momentarily off-balance by the riposte but she recovered quickly. "You may supervise Jessica's school work. I consider any other involvement inappropriate."

Again, Sandra parried with a question. "Mrs. Hope, are you here as a concerned parent or in a professional capacity?"

Roberta would not lose her footing a second time.

"That is all I came to say. I'm sure the matter of your professional conduct —" Roberta paused to stress *professional* — "is between you and your department. Thank you for your time, Dr. Ross."

The door closed again, the implied threat delivered and left hanging in the air. Sandra held onto her pencil a moment longer, then dropped it. Internal fingers, clenched around her temper, loosened slowly. Anger, held so long in check, reared and kicked.

How quickly the alarms sounded when a barrier was breached, she thought. How quickly the defending armies rushed to reinforce protocol. For years she had confined herself to form, and to what end? So that she could dress tastefully at cocktail parties.

Sandra thought about risk, real and perceived. What happened when you couldn't tell one from the other? She inhaled sharply, trying for calm. She had tried to compromise, wading the shallows with her back to the breakers. But the answers she needed ran deeper than ethics or form. She would have to swim and risk the tide.

She turned to the window, her class momentarily forgotten. The live oak presided over the view, a silent witness passing judgment only on the weather. Sandra pressed her fingers to the glass. California offered no seasons and the time had come for her to define her own salvation. The color of winter, Sandra decided, was the exact shade of leaves on an oak tree — silvery gray, always green.

\* \* \* \* \*

Sandra couldn't remember a word of her lecture. "Get a hold of yourself," she muttered.

There would be no point in defending her career if she couldn't get the job done. She strode down a corridor on the way to her office. Lost in thought, she passed the faculty conference room before the voices registered.

"I am not entirely satisfied with this situation."

Recognizing Roberta Hope's formal tone, Sandra halted just past the doorway. On any other day she would have continued down the corridor. Instead, she crossed her arms, ready to add eavesdropping to her list of new sins.

"Of course not." Sam's reassuring voice was unmistakable. "You've helped us put together a solid department," he said. "Give us time to get the job done."

"Must I remind you that we are on a timeline?" Roberta's tone held more threat than question.

Sam responded calmly. "The semester's not over."

Roberta said icily, "You have one priority. Don't lose sight of it."

"Of course not."

The voices faded as Sam and Roberta moved farther from the doorway. Sandra heard the hum of conversation but could no longer follow the words. She headed toward her office, her thoughts ricocheting. She glanced at her desk. Ungraded papers stared back in silent accusation. They would have to wait a while longer. The phone shrilled.

"Yes."

"Oh, God, you've gone monosyllabic."

"Hello, Amy."

"One of my meetings is cancelled. Do you want coffee?"

"Please."

"Meet me in twenty minutes."

The café chattered with a late-afternoon crowd, the West Coast equivalent of teatime. A useful ritual, Sandra thought as she carried her cup to an empty table. Life contained so many harmless and comforting routines.

She had wrapped herself in insulating habit, chinking up the cracks of anxiety with purpose and detail. She had hemmed her skirts and balanced her checkbook, staving off panic, surrounding herself with a moat of decorum. A long time ago she had glimpsed an inner core, then built her life to protect it. Now, as she took a second look inside, she suspected the core might not crack after all.

"You look lost in morbid thought." Amy set an over-tall glass of espresso and steamed milk on the table.

"Not so lost," Sandra said.

"Are you having a religious conversion? It's almost time for finals."

Sandra contemplated her friend. "You're such an unlikely confessor."

Amy's eyes narrowed.

"Stop squinting. You look like you're about to pounce."

Amy asked, "Are you sure you're not prey?"

"I'm sure."

"Good. Then let's stop talking in metaphor. Do the words *Jessica Hope* and *professional suicide* come to mind?"

Sandra smiled. "Your perceptions remain unchallenged."

"Jesus, Sandra. Call nine-one-one." Amy shook her head. "Rumors are flying. Do you know what you're doing?"

"I can't justify what I'm doing, but I'm starting to figure out what I want."

"Terrific. That's a fine position to defend."

"I won't defend it."

Amy leaned into the table. "And just what exactly have you decided that you want?"

Sandra said evenly, "Jay Hope."

Amy moaned. "Oh, God. Don't call me as a character witness, Sandra. I should get myself as far away from this as possible. I can't condone it."

"No, I wouldn't ask you to."

"I should have known," Amy said with another shake of her head. "You quiet ones. There's always danger under the surface."

"Amy, I don't want to lose your friendship, but I'll understand if you need to take some distance for a while."

"I should write you off." Amy sighed. "There's just this little matter of respect. I don't know what the hell you think you're doing, Sandra, but I still respect you."

Sandra said earnestly, "Thank you."

"Look, don't fill me in on the graphic details. Yet. Probably the less I know, the better. However —" Amy smiled — "I'll be happy to read your diaries when this is over."

"Sorry, Amy. No diaries."

Amy looked at her for a long moment. "You don't frown as much as you used to."

Sandra broke into laughter. "Did you just give me your blessing?"

Amy shrugged.

"No warnings about smoke alarms or bullets?"

"It won't look great on a résumé," Amy said with another sigh, "but passion won't kill you."

"No," Sandra replied, "and neither will the truth."

Amy leaned across the table and covered Sandra's hand with her own. "Finding the truth," she said. "Now there's a trick."


Darkness obscured the hills by the time Sandra returned home. Amy had offered to drive but she refused, knowing the bus ride would help her think. Jay's business was closed for the day, her home number unlisted.

Walking the few blocks to Kozy's restaurant, Sandra waited at a table in the back. After a moment Kozy sat down beside her. Sandra made her request and watched Kozy disappear into the kitchen. A waitress came and placed a cup of tea on the table, then left her alone. Kozy returned shortly, handing Sandra a slip of paper with an address and phone number.

"Thank you."

Kozy nodded, leaving Sandra to show herself out. Sandra returned home and dialed the number.

"Hi." Jay's voice was warm on the line. "Kozy said you might call."

"Hello, Jay. Your shop was closed."

"Sandra, are you okay?"

"Yes, of course. Jay, I'll be leaving for Boston at the end of the semester. Will you come with me?"

"I think I'll have my paper finished by then."

"I'm sorry, Jay. I won't be able to recommend your project to the department. I'll continue to assist if you wish, but you'll have to present the paper by yourself."

After a short silence Jay asked, "Does this mean you're no longer my supervisor?"

"Officially, no. I'm not."

"Then may I take this as an invitation?"

Sandra felt herself smile. "Yes. You may."

Jay arrived a while later. They undressed in silence and made love without words. Sandra held Jay softly until she felt a saltwater wetness against her skin. Then, as she had done before, she turned to put Jay beneath her, rocking them both to a warm release.

When they were resting in the darkness Jay asked, "Do you want to tell me what happened?"

Sandra propped herself on one elbow, looking down at Jay, her fingers tracing shadows along a shoulder. "I don't think I've felt this carefree since I was a child. I used to run along the beach and play in the waves." She smiled. "I haven't done that for a very long time."

Jay reached to brush gray strands of hair from Sandra's face. "Why did you stop?"

"Too many memories got in the way. I began to be afraid the waves would pull me out to sea."

"Are you afraid now?"

"Your mother paid me a visit."

Jay groaned. "What did she threaten?"

"My tenure, I believe." Sandra felt Jay's arm tense under her fingers.

"She's used to the university rolling over."

Sandra gave a low laugh. "Well, we have certainly rolled over, darling, although probably not in the way she intended."

Jay sat up. "You may not be my supervisor, but I'm still registered as a student. You're giving the school a lot of ammunition."

"I don't take kindly to extortion."

"So flunk me. Why put your career on the line?"

Sandra thought again about risk. She thought she was beginning to understand how Californians could live along the coast, perched on a double edge of beauty and destruction.

She said, "You convinced me that passion is more important than safety."

Jay kissed her softly. "I'm sorry I can't protect you. I have no sense of propriety."

But Sandra had finally accepted that there was no hope of protection. Society tamed nature as best it could and enforced its chosen laws. Institutions injected the values, leaving victims to develop immunities or suffer in exile. In the end, everyone suffered the exposure. Only a few hearty souls truly embraced the elements.

Sandra switched on a lamp and swung her legs over the edge of the bed. She stood at the full-length mirror in her bedroom, gazing at her naked reflection. She had thought security would be protection enough, but fear demanded a compliance she couldn't provide. She knew the answers but refused to let them speak. Trapped, they kept her awake at night and burned deeply, like poison. Her reflection stared back, daring her to find the antidote.

# Chapter 14

Sandra arrived on campus earlier than usual. Classes seemed alive with static. Students picked up their pace through the corridors as the semester hurried toward completion. Barry Donovan burst unannounced into Sandra's office.

"Are you crazy?" He lost the end of his accusation in a squeak.

Barry was almost turning in circles, pacing nervously across the small office. A rat on a wheel, Sandra thought uncharitably.

He stopped spinning and stared accusingly at

Sandra. "I want you to know that Mrs. Hope came to see me."

Sandra sat back in her chair and crossed her arms.

"Off the record," he continued, "she has no intention of filing a complaint. At least not yet. You should know, however, there is talk of indiscretion."

Sandra said firmly, "No one has any intention of indiscretion, on or off the record."

"Damnit, stop parroting my words. I'm not stupid, Sandra, and neither are you. You've ruined a great opportunity."

"Great for whom, Barry. For you?" Sandra kept her voice low. "Make your career moves by yourself."

He stamped his foot. "I'll take this to the department. You jeopardize all of us with your poor judgment."

"I'm sure you'll do what you think best, as will I."

"God damn it, Sandra." He began to whine, "It could have been so good."

Sandra stood and leaned across her desk. "You may not be stupid, Barry, but you're an ass. Now get the hell out of my office."

Barry opened his mouth to speak but Sandra glared a warning. He clenched his teeth, slamming the door shut behind him. Not her most eloquent diction, Sandra reflected, but effective. She didn't think about Barry again until faculty meeting.

Moving quickly through the agenda, Sam asked, "New business?"

Barry placed both hands on the table and began to stand. He apparently planned to wage a full-scale presentation.

Audrey met him before he was half out of his seat. "Sit down, Barry."

"I beg your pardon."

"I said, sit down." Audrey leveled him a look usually reserved for the most arrogant of students. She said evenly, "I'm tired of your habit of superseding our discussions." Looking around the table, she continued, "I, for one, am swamped with work. I suggest we table any new business until next semester. Agreed?"

Heads nodded enthusiastically and the room emptied quickly. Barry dragged out, wilted in defeat.

In the hallway, Sandra turned to Audrey. "Thank you."

"Have you been to the rose gardens lately?"

"Not since my first visit."

"Saturday, then. If the weather holds." Audrey turned away without further comment.

Sam matched his steps to Sandra's as she headed back to her office. He said, "Barry's an ass."

"My words exactly." Sandra tried for a smile.

"Sandra." Sam slowed his pace, keeping his eyes focused on the corridor straight ahead.

"Spit it out, Sam."

"A lot of department funding comes through the Hope Foundation. Surely you can understand that Roberta Hope has a great deal of influence."

"And there are certain conditions which satisfy that influence, correct?"

Sandra quickened her steps and Sam hurried to keep up.

"You've dropped Jay's supervision. Why?"

"I found I could no longer work within the given parameters."

Sam rubbed his eyes. "If I had any proof of the accusations Barry is making, I'd fire you on the spot."

Sandra felt exhausted. "Do what you must."

"That's it? Do what I must? Is that all you're going to say?"

"I can no longer rely on form, Sam. I'm sorry."

"Following form is what this place is about." Anger resonated in his voice. "And form requires compromise."

"I've been warned about compromise." Sandra eyed him. "Just what kind of deal did you make?"

"I make deals for funding, what do you think?"

Sandra gasped as realization crystallized. "You set this up." She stopped walking. "I thought you made a mistake in hiring me, but I was a political appointment after all, wasn't I?" She faced him. "Did Roberta promise you more funding? Is that how you finally managed to expand the department?" Sandra clenched her jaw. "You hired me in exchange for grant money. What made you think Jay would choose me to be her supervisor?"

"It was a gamble. I didn't have a lot of time. Of course, your inexperience is an asset. Jay hates authority. And I had to find someone from out of town."

Sandra's mind raced. "I must have been perfect. No connections to the foundation — that would entice Jay." She glared at Sam. "You wanted an older teacher as well, right? A cautious new professor to go

143

along with the plan, someone who wouldn't jeopardize a chance at tenure." When Sam remained silent she snapped, "How can you be so sure she'll turn over the money?"

"Who else is she going to give it to? Her family has always supported education. Besides, she never cared about the money."

"And money justifies the motives, is that it?"

Sam shot back, "My job is about money. It wouldn't hurt you to remember that your job depends on it, too. Damnit, Sandra, money and education are inseparable. Get used to it."

"Damn me if you like," Sandra said firmly, "but I reserve the right to choose my own religion."

Sam sighed and lowered his voice. "Does Jay intend to complete the project?"

"She said she will. That means little, Sam, and you know it. Even if you give her advanced academic standing, can you keep her in school for the next year and a half to finish the degree?"

"You tell me, will she do it?"

"The decision is hers. It always has been."

Sam cleared his throat. "You're a good teacher, Sandra. I wish I could ignore that fact, but I can't." He rubbed a hand thoughtfully against his chin. "Have something ready for publication by the end of spring semester. If you don't, I can't even begin to save your job."

Sandra watched as he walked away, once again the chairman, confident in his ability to compromise. She went to her office, taking what comfort she could find in the oak's persistent leaves.

# Chapter 15

Saturday dawned crisp and clear. Sandra waited on a bench, her jacket zipped against wind blowing inland from the water. She could find no shelter from her thoughts, however, and they broke across her in a whirlwind. She chased accusations and justifications like torn scraps of paper.

She knew that a relationship with a student defied her own convictions. She had subscribed to social codes and made them her own, but she no longer trusted conventional wisdom. Jay seemed content to ignore the rules, but even Jay's careful defenses were not impregnable. Sandra, having taken refuge for so long behind the walls of fair behavior, now found the stones unforgiving and oppressive. She might have the strength to tear down one block, but when the whole structure collapsed, then where would she live?

Sandra looked up to find Audrey standing beside the bench, also wrapped in a jacket against the chill. Even the rose bushes had succumbed to winter, Sandra noticed, their blossoms gone for the season.

"You never did tell me about your hobbies," Sandra said as Audrey sat down. "Besides roses."

"I collect sculpture. I have some lovely wood, carved locally."

"Jay."

Audrey looked at her. "Have you seen her work?"

"No. I saw one piece, I think, that's all."

They sat for a while, then Audrey said, "You seem to have taken my words literally. I asked you to look into her heart, did I not?"

"I appreciate what you did at the meeting. I'm not going to ask for approval."

Audrey remained silent.

Sandra tucked her hands into her pockets. "How long have you known her?"

"I've been trying to get her to drop out of school for years."

Sandra said slowly, "Teachers and students share an educational contract. I've always believed in it."

"I'm more concerned with the covenant the student holds with herself," Audrey replied. "You may be in violation of some standard or another, but what if there's a greater lesson to be learned?"

"I told you before," Sandra said, "I'm not that arrogant. And I won't rationalize action by saying it's for a greater good."

"It's obvious that you teach to inspire."

Sandra grimaced. "Joan of Arc was an inspiration and look where it got her. Besides, all of my relatives are lawyers who teach respect for the law."

Audrey gave Sandra a dry smile. "If you want to wait until the laws are in your favor," she suggested, "consider the concept of reincarnation." Audrey waved a dismissive hand. "You're an historian. Heretics and saviors have always been judged by the truths they claim. In the end, truth will outlast religion."

Sandra sighed. "I need to teach something besides religion. In the meantime, I'm going to Boston."

Audrey seemed content to watch the bay. Finally she said, "Go to Boston. Have a nice holiday. Just remember that your students will be waiting for you here."

"I'm not sure how much, if anything, will still be here for me."

"Have more confidence, Sandra." Audrey remained intent on the water. "Has it occurred to you that I'm jealous?"

Sandra stared in frank astonishment. "When you fell out of the ivory tower, Audrey, just how hard did you hit?"

"I didn't fall very far, I'm afraid. Jay dropped my class. I made the mistake of visiting her home."

"She's learned your bad habits."

"I fell in love with her wood and offered to sponsor her through art school."

"She didn't accept, I take it."

"She laughed in my face," Audrey replied calmly.

"That was it, nothing else happened. She started the antiques business shortly afterwards and I called her a coward."

"Oh, Audrey . . ." Sandra's voice trailed off in dismay.

"Yes, I took her decisions personally. The last thing she told me was that I'd made a pass at the wrong Hope. She indicated I'd have had better luck with her mother."

"Ouch."

"Roberta Hope," Audrey continued, "has been using Sam for a long time. I suspect that everyone, Jay included, got a bit more than they bargained for in you."

"I'm not innocent."

"I didn't say that."

"Audrey, why did you stop growing roses?"

Audrey stood and looked at her. "Perhaps it's time I began another garden." She smiled briefly. "I'll see you next semester."

Sandra stayed on the bench after Audrey's departure. Questions paraded before her like a steady stream of supplicants, whispering softly, seeking answers, saying as much as a vow of silence would allow. Fear was her father's legacy, and she would have to go to New England to face her harsh inheritance. In spite of Audrey's assurances, Sandra knew that if she failed to define the fear, there would be no reason to return.

Sandra sat with her hands hidden from the wind, thinking of Berkeley and thinking of Boston. Not even Jay knew that she'd bought a one-way ticket.

# Chapter 16

Sandra sat curled in the armchair in Jay's office at the back of the store. The space heater hummed and her pencil scratched softly, marking passages and noting comments, page after page. She always wrote in her books, which meant she had to buy them and not borrow. It made little difference that *The Missions of California* was for her own enjoyment; outlining thoughts on paper came as naturally to her as eating or drinking.

The door opened and Jay peeked in. "It's almost closing time. Are you hungry?"

Sandra nodded. "I'll cook for us tonight."

Jay grinned and turned back to the shop, leaving the office door slightly ajar. Jay had already closed the window blinds in front, but a knock sounded. She heard Jay unlatch the front door but couldn't see who entered. Sandra bent over her book, but the conversation diverted her attention.

"Hello, Mother. I was just closing."

"Jessica, hello. I won't keep you long."

Sandra sat unmoving, letting the book fall silently shut in her lap. A sofa protested against a settling weight. Sandra pictured Jay trying to fit herself onto an early American love seat. Jay was always too tall for her antiques.

Roberta Hope paced in Sandra's line of sight before her footsteps creaked away to the other side of the store. Roberta seemed reluctant to make herself comfortable on her daughter's merchandise.

"What can I do for you, Mother?"

The tension in Jay's voice carried easily to the back office. Sandra remained motionless, weighing the options of exposure and confrontation. She chose silence, uncertain of her decision, unwilling to intrude.

"I came to offer my assistance." Roberta's trumpet-like tone rang with the sound of battle. If there was a note of sympathy, Sandra couldn't hear it. "It's no secret that your supervisor has abandoned your research project," she continued. "I am prepared to help."

Jay sighed. "Is that an indication of your confidence in my academic ability?"

Roberta said stiffly, "I want to be sure that you have every advantage."

"And what do you consider advantageous?" Jay sounded tired.

"Dr. Ross is not a reliable resource. However, I am aware of several supervisors with excellent credentials who will be happy to work with you."

Sandra clenched her jaw against a sudden urge to scream. To calm herself, she prepared a mental list of adjectives for Roberta Hope, in alphabetical order.

*Acrimonious*, she began a silent chant. *Base, condescending.* The sharp sound of Jay's boots scraping against the floor underscored *dangerous*.

"Mother." Jay was clearly angry. "My career as a student depends on one thing — your non-interference. Don't even think about manipulating my schoolwork, or I'll give up the trust and send a press release to the NRA."

*Astute.* Sandra began a list for Jay. *Bold, commendable.*

"Mother, one more thing. Dr. Ross is an excellent resource. That point isn't even up for debate."

Sandra held her breath as the front door opened, then closed. "Damn," she whispered, exhaling. She lost her place in the alphabet and repeated, "Damn."

She heard Jay cross the room and then the door to the small office was pushed wide open.

"Still feel like cooking?" Jay wore a weary smile.

Sandra could only nod. She was suddenly at a loss for words.

Jay opened a bottle of wine while Sandra vigorously sliced onions. A mound of grated cheese spilled over a plate. Sandra's knife danced along the butcher's block and mushrooms lined up quickly behind the onions.

"Slow down," Jay said. "I won't starve."

"Not if I have anything to say about it."

Sandra stretched pizza dough into the shape of a disc, then tossed it into the air, catching it expertly on floured hands.

Jay gave a low whistle. "Impressive."

Sandra turned away and settled the dough onto a pan. "I feel a bit like a coward."

"You're no coward. Confronting my mother would be crazy, depressing, and not very effective."

Sandra layered ingredients thickly on the pizza. "You forgot a and b."

"What?"

"Oh, never mind."

Sandra dusted the pie with oregano. Long fingers sneaked past her to steal a fat, cheese-covered mushroom.

"Stop that." She swatted at Jay's hand and the fingers caught her and pulled her close. "Set the table," she scolded, tasting olive oil on Jay's lips.

"In a minute."

But Sandra turned and pulled away. She reached to untie her apron and the ends snagged in a knot. Once more she felt Jay's fingers.

"Hold still."

Sandra stopped pulling and leaned her head back against Jay's shoulder. "Come with me to Boston, darling."

"This is a busy season for me. And I know you have friends to visit. Use the time for yourself, Sandra." The apron came free and Jay lifted it over her head. "I love the way you cook."

Sandra pushed the pizza into the oven while Jay built a fire. When the meal was ready, they neglected the table and sat on the sofa, sharing dinner.

Sandra asked, "How will you spend the holidays?"

"Working furiously until the eleventh hour. Then I'll put in a family appearance. With any luck, I'll be too tired to be embarrassed by my mother." Jay licked cheese from her fingers. "And Jonathan always gives a giant New Year's party. With Michael it was a tradition, but Jon insisted on doing it himself this year. The party is always the real celebration for me."

Sandra picked at her food. "Have you always had conflicts with your mother?"

"My mother used to laugh, believe it or not." Jay paused between bites. "She and my father were happy for a while. I remember one time, I was pretty little, I wandered into my parents' bedroom when my mother was getting ready for a bath. The bathroom door was open and I saw her sinking into bubbles. It looked like magic. I think I used to be in awe of her."

"When did things change?"

"I was thirteen when I realized they were having affairs. My father eventually took his share of the stocks and bonds and left, but not before I learned that my mother has an enormous capacity to cause pain."

Jay smiled. "Lately I've been thinking that it might be a good thing if she had another affair. It's been so long since I've had anything at all in common with her."

"She has a hard time accepting you."

"I'm still a disappointment to her."

Sandra set her plate aside. She pulled both knees up to her chin and circled them with her arms, watching Jay in the firelight, enjoying the play of light and shadow.

"It was hardest when I started the business," Jay continued. "She threatened to cut me off and I told her I didn't care. I told her I had plenty of furniture to invest in and that by comparison she was a difficult bargain." Jay's eyes sparkled. "I think that got her attention."

"Is there any possibility of a reconciliation?"

Jay shrugged. "She really does want me to be happy, but I don't think she knows who I am. I'm partly to blame for that, I guess." She added quietly, "There are worse things than being an outcast."

"Name one."

"Fear," Jay said seriously. "Fear makes us outcasts from ourselves."

Sandra moved closer to her, seeking her strong embrace. Comfort still eluded her. She had never intended to confront her father's ghost directly. But it had tapped her on the shoulder and compelled her to turn; in turning there was recognition, and recognition required a greeting. She could no longer pretend that the past didn't matter.

Jay's fingers found and massaged tense muscle. "Did you turn in the semester grades?"

"Yes, thank goodness. I'm leaving tomorrow. If you want any help with your paper, now's the time to ask."

"I've got your notes and a two week grace period before it's due. You can read the finished product when you get back."

Sandra sighed. "This may be a long trip."

"Do you want to try to get some sleep?"

Sandra pushed the remnants of dinner aside and pulled Jay into her arms. "Sleep is the last thing I want right now."

# Chapter 17

Sandra turned up the collar on her jacket, its thin, West Coast lining no match for the sharp New England air. She breathed deeply and exhaled a cloud of vapor. A circling car made a dive for a spot of curb and Alix waved a long arm through the passenger window. Sophie, short and muscular, jumped out, ignoring honks from other lane-swimming drivers. She tossed Sandra's bag easily into the trunk and gave Sandra a breath-shortening squeeze.

"Good to see you. Hop in the back and talk to Alix while I get us out of here."

Alix, a tall and lanky graphic artist, referred to herself as a matter of too much arm and leg, lamenting the lack of Avon products to disguise them. Turning in her seat, she gave Sandra a thorough once-over.

"You have a lot of explaining to do, sweetheart. Your communications have been terse, to say the least."

Sandra relaxed into the back seat, enjoying the frank, choppy accents of her friends. "It's good to see you both."

Sophie out-raced the cab drivers and soon had them past the worst of the airport traffic. Alix brushed a stray curl out of her lover's eyes, a simple, intimate gesture.

Alix said, "I hope you're hungry. Sophie's been cooking."

Sophie's brusque exterior couldn't hide her generous, energetic nature, but it disguised a sensitive poet. To the dismay of Alix's more feminist friends, Sophie worked as an engineer for a defense contractor. Her latest design project, according to a letter from Alix, included a grenade launcher.

If her work had caused a stir in the community, it was nothing compared to the uproar when Sophie first disappeared into the New Hampshire mountains with a hunting rifle. Sophie never engaged her critics. Her mother, she had once confided to Sandra, crossed the border illegally from Mexico to California to deliver her child. Sophie took her American birth certificate and moved north and east into an enviable income bracket.

"Your friends supported the laws that helped me learn a trade and get a job," she told Sandra. "Now I earn a living, I own a home, and I have a freezer full of food. Let them scream. I've never been so happy."

Watching Alix steal a kiss from Sophie as they puttered around a pint-sized kitchen, Sandra admired their contentment.

"Leave me alone in here," Sophie growled. "Go. Entertain."

Alix handed Sandra a glass of wine, carrying a beer for herself. Wide, low chairs furnished the living room and brightly colored pillows crowded every corner. An enormous aquarium stretched along one wall.

Alix said, "You've been too quiet, you stopped writing, you haven't mentioned your work, and you've been watching Sophie and me like a vulture. What's her name?"

Sandra gave a startled laugh. "I have a friend in the psychology department. She'd love to meet you."

"Are you two gossiping? I want to hear the gossip," Sophie yelled from the kitchen. "Don't tell the good stuff till I get there."

Alix raised an eyebrow in exasperation and raised her voice in turn. "You kicked us out of the kitchen, dear. Make up your mind."

"Talk about the weather. I need five minutes in here."

"What's for dinner?" Sandra asked.

"Seafood and salsa. So, how's the weather out there?"

"Mild and beautiful. I miss the real stuff."

"Meaning ice, snow, cold feet and hazardous driving."

"Colorful leaves and soft, falling flakes."

Alix gave Sandra a measured look. "Are you writing?"

"No, thinking too much."

Sophie came out of the kitchen balancing a tray of food and an armload of plates. Sandra jumped up to help while Alix cleared magazines from the coffee table.

"We'll eat in here," Sophie declared. "Kick your shoes off."

Sandra had never known her friends to eat in their dining room. Sophie tended to use the large table for blueprints.

There were warm tortillas and strips of grilled shark, diced scallion and fresh lime salsa. Sophie's cooking echoed her life, full of enthusiasm and surprising subtlety. The fish tasted tender and smoky.

"It's like chicken," Alix said.

Sophie scowled. "It's shark. Chickens have beaks, sharks have teeth."

Sandra licked lime juice from her fingers, thinking of avocadoes. "It's delicious."

"Well." Alix picked up her beer. "That covers the food and the weather. If you don't tell me about the rest of your life, I'm going to break out one of Sophie's hunting weapons and threaten innocent people."

"I don't keep ammunition in the house," Sophie said. "You know that."

"Sophie, honey," Alix said, "shut up."

Sandra spoke into the moment of quiet. "She's a student. It's serious."

One of Sophie's grenades, Sandra thought, would have exploded more softly.

Alix found her voice first. "A student? Sandra, are you out of your mind?"

"Yes. No."

"Well, it's about time you had some fun," Sophie said. "If you have to break a few rules to do it, so much the better."

Alix glared at her lover. "Her job could be at stake."

"I'm afraid my job may be at stake either way," Sandra admitted. "Her family is wealthy and her mother pulls a lot of purse strings at the university. She pretty much tried to bribe me to make sure her daughter gets a degree."

"So you refused the bribe and took the girl." Alix shook her head. "How can you have so much integrity and throw ethics out the window?"

"Situational ethics." Sophie spoke as though delivering a new commandment. "Honor your own truth."

"Sophie, we know Sandra's honorable, but they don't give credit for personal growth."

Sandra listened as her friends argued the same points she had already debated. After a moment, she interrupted. "I think I just got tired of being cautious."

"It's about time," Sophie said again. Leaning over the low table, she kissed Sandra, a gesture of compassion. "I've heard all I need to hear, honey. You know what you're doing." She picked up an armload of dishes and headed for the kitchen. "You two can talk all night. I have to work tomorrow."

Alix moved to sit beside Sandra, wrapping long arms around her in a friendly hug. "I love you, Sandra. I don't want to see you get burned."

Sandra smiled at the familiar imagery. "I've been warned about playing with fire. To tell you the truth, I feel like I'm thawing out. I welcome the warmth."

Alix gave her another squeeze and sighed. "All right. So, tell me about her."

They talked until they were both yawning, reminiscing about old friends, sharing the kind of insights about life that appear late at night — brilliant thoughts destined to fade at daylight. Finally Alix unfolded herself from the pillows.

"The guest room is made up. Sleep as late as you want. I'll meet you tomorrow for lunch." Alix paused, one hand draped across her hip. "Are you sleeping at all these days?"

Sandra asked, "Is the wine still in storage?"

"Sophie's tempted to use it for target practice."

"She watches too many westerns."

"So, do you want some? Don't make me go through my co-dependent act twice."

"I haven't decided what to do with the wine, yet. And no, I don't need any tonight."

In spite of her brave words, Sandra tossed restlessly for hours. She dozed as the sky painted itself pink with dawn.

\* \* \* \* \*

Sandra and Alix strolled through the Friday Haymarket crowds. Voices paraded around them, laughter mingling with muted arguments as prices were fixed and broken, repaired again for each new customer. By noon the open market stalls were busy with tourists and locals.

Sandra, enjoying her leisure, felt like a stranger in her old neighborhood. The mixed aromas of garlic and olive oil scented the breeze in the narrow streets. Alix paused in front of a North End restaurant, its windows lightly steamed against the December air. A steady rush of business-suited men and women crowded quickly into small tables.

"Come on." Alix pulled Sandra by the arm. "Let's grab a spot while we can."

They ate mussels steamed in wine, and pasta tossed with fresh basil and garlic.

"Sophie will be wild if I come home smelling like garlic," Alix complained. "I'll have to buy breath mints."

"Mints for you, flowers for her?" Sandra joked.

"You laugh. Most people worry about lovers coming home with lipstick on their collars. Mine gets upset if I eat out without her."

"You two have done well together," Sandra said. "It's clear you're happy."

"I am happy." Alix sighed. "It took a few years to believe it would last. I don't think either one of us counted on long-term domesticity."

"What makes it work for you?"

"Hell, Sandra, ask me a hard one." Alix mulled for a moment, then said, "It took us a while to figure out that all of our fights were about the same thing." Sandra shook her head and Alix explained,

"You know, someone's feeling smothered so they get mad about the way the bills get paid. Someone else feels abandoned so they complain about the toothpaste cap. The scenarios change but the underlying issues are always the same."

"How do you recognize the real problem?"

Alix grinned. "When we both ended up crying in the bathroom for the fourth fight in a row, that was a clue. Buying a toothpaste pump helped, too." She rested her chin on her hand. "You have to get past the surface issues to the stuff underneath."

Sandra heard Jay's voice whisper, *Underneath the surface, love is very soft, very simple.*

"I have to get back to the studio." Alix's words interrupted the memory. "See you tonight?"

Sandra pulled herself back to the present. "Yes. I'll be leaving for the Cape in the morning."

Alix kissed her cheek, laughing when Sandra reminded her to buy gum. Sandra made a determined effort to reacquaint herself with Boston's subway and found her way back to Cambridge's bookstores. Alix's words followed her through familiar streets.

Her fights with herself were always the same. The demons she had pushed out of sight bobbed to the surface insistently, and with increasing frequency. They were hungry. She had starved them with silence, refusing to nourish fear with despair. Now the fight rolled toward her like a wave across the water. No one else could mediate her past. Sandra walked briskly through New England's winter, preparing to do battle with her oldest foe.

# Chapter 18

Sandra rented a car and drove to Cape Cod for Christmas. Her brother filled his house every year with a confusion of cousins, their spouses and children. Torn between familiarity and awkwardness, Sandra was too academic to be dismissed, too coarse in her solitude for easy acceptance. She took refuge in ritual as gifts were exchanged, food consumed, holiday habits performed and discarded.

Brian cornered her in the hallway. "Have you found a fairy tale in the sun? Prince Charming with a tan, perhaps?"

Sandra smiled. "Brian, I'm only going to say this once. I prefer the princess."

Her brother's eyes widened briefly before his courtroom polish came to the rescue. He drained his drink in one long swallow. "So this is how the West was won. Fill me in on the details later. In the meantime, stay away from Uncle Brad."

Sandra laughed and toasted his already departing back. Every family had a Brad, someone who made it a duty to determine the family values and careers. Each generation entrenched habit and defended custom, sacrificing preference on the alter of tradition. Uncle Bradford also practiced law.

Sandra remembered her father sitting at his easel on weekends, seemingly unaware that the family considered him a flop.

*If I could only paint the light on the water I would be happy,* he told her.

And he filled the house with oil and canvas until the day he put his paints in the garbage and walked into the waves. Brian and Sandra were packed off to college. They learned to excel academically, refusing extracurricular activities lest the waves claim them too.

At the end of the evening, Brian rocked slowly on the porch swing, his sturdy legs keeping time with creaking wood. Guests had patted cheeks and departed, family members slept, saturated in post-holiday contentment. Sandra pulled a chair close to the wood stove, wrapping a blanket around her shoulders. The enclosed porch offered drafty protection from the brittle air.

Brian said, "I thought I might hang some of his paintings."

Sandra looked at her brother, his features an inexact mirror for her own expressions. They both resembled their mother. Only Uncle Brad had the face of their father. It was perhaps the cruelest of memories to find the form of a loved one in the person who most wanted to forget. Her father's younger brother remained on guard against the defective family branch, unwilling to let it bud again in the wrong direction. Brad had no patience for deviance. He considered the misbegotten limb tragically but inevitably severed.

Sandra never even knew who to blame. She could more easily feel anger at her mother for failing to protect the man she had married, as if such protection were possible. It was easier now to simply feel the sadness.

"I think of him more now than I have in years," Sandra admitted. "I thought by moving away I'd finally forget."

"I thought by living in his house I might replace him." Brian smiled sadly.

The expression pierced Sandra. Her father used to smile that way, as if humor never quite escaped the hurt. She turned in her chair to watch the water. The waves rolled and receded, returning with the tide. One could be pushed back to land as easily as pulled out to sea. Maybe the tides were indecisive after all.

Gathering her blanket, Sandra moved to sit beside Brian in the swing, holding her breath as it creaked under their combined weight.

"Whoa, steady there." Brian laughed.

"I don't think we've sat here together since we were kids," Sandra joked, "and you always used to push me off."

"The prodigal daughter returns, pulling the house down around her."

"Nonsense. You'd be surprised at what a house can survive. They're built to weather amazing forces."

"Taken up the history of architecture?" Brian teased lightly.

"Everyone in California's an expert on architecture. They feel safer in earthquakes because they understand foundations."

"The Golden State seems to suit you."

"If you want more information, ask directly."

"You're not allowed to withhold evidence."

"Convict me."

The banter came easily, but Sandra resisted the habit. She had already braced for the fight. Why not speak the final truth?

"Why do you think he killed himself, Brian?"

"It's a long time now to ask that question."

Sandra said impatiently, "I spent fifteen years trying to forget, ten years trying to understand, and the last few trying not to do it myself."

"Jesus, Sandra." Brian halted, then confessed, "Yeah, I think about it, too. I don't know why he did it. All I remember is one day I came home and the house was empty." An edge of anger crept into Brian's voice. "I hated the emptiness. He was always so quiet. I didn't know it would feel so empty without him."

"I think he wanted to die because he was always

trying to capture beauty, but when it touched him he only felt pain."

Brian touched her hand. "He really loved you."

"He loved us both."

"I know, but he had high hopes for you. You were quiet, like him, so intense."

Sandra felt a swell of tears and searched again for safety.

"I guess it's nice to know someone in the family will carry on the deviant gene." She smiled, trying for lightness.

Brian responded fiercely, "Just do it happily, not tragically."

Sandra laced her fingers through his. "Happiness is about freedom, don't you think?"

"What do you mean?"

"He gave us the freedom to make our own decisions. He broke the rules first."

"I always thought that meant I had to be extra careful with all the rest."

"Me too."

Brian asked, "What changed your mind?"

"I got tired of the fear." Sandra squinted at the dark horizon. "And a whole state dedicated to defying earthquakes. If the world can survive its own tremendous strength surely we can survive our puny flaws."

Brian looked around the house and surrounding beach. "So, should I sell this place and move west?"

"Don't you dare."

He patted her shoulder and stretched. "Goodnight, Sandra. Maybe we'll look through those paintings tomorrow."

She listened to his footsteps sounding with certainty in the hallway, then she rose to place another log in the stove. She sat for a while, watching the water, listening to the untiring tide. She dozed, then slept, dreaming of oil paints spreading on water, a thick stain of color refusing to be washed out to sea.

She opened her eyes as dawn touched the earth, pink and orange spilling carelessly out of heaven to play in the waves. Rubbing a crick in her neck, she left the blanket on the porch and braved the cold for a brisk walk on the beach.

She had feared the hell that claimed her father — not a pit of brimstone but of promises, always out of reach. Self-doubt towered on the shoreline, sculpted like a monolith, an ocean creature made of salt and desperation. Uncertain of herself, she had framed the narrowest of paths, fearing always that she might follow her father's footsteps into the Atlantic ocean.

Sandra looked across the water and it was there in an instant, a flash of sun, a glistening on the surface. The light on the water offered no promise, only possibilities. As she watched, the light winked and faded, and then the water rolled toward her without highlight. It didn't matter; she knew what she had seen.

Waves jumped against the wind and chased a breeze against the beach. Fear receded on the tide. Sandra pulled her hands out of her pockets and stared at knuckles ridged like whitecaps, the lines on her palms drawn with permanence. She returned to the house and found her way to coffee and a shower, then she called the airline for a plane ticket home.

* * * * *

Light snow fell in Boston as Sophie greeted her.

"I can never get used to the snow," Sophie said. "Do you miss it?"

"I'm getting used to fog," Sandra replied.

They drank coffee, sitting by the window to watch the storm.

"Alix is running errands, she'll be home soon."

"Sophie," Sandra asked, "how do you learn to live without the rules?"

"Everyone assumes that when you fall from grace you have to go straight to hell," Sophie stated. "You don't."

"No? Then what happens?"

"You live your own life. That's all you have."

Sandra watched branches bend with the force of wind. Her life had room, now, for new growth. She wanted to send her own roots deep underground, regardless of the boundaries on the surface. She was ready to live with fire and water in a state that built heaven over hell, knowing that she could redefine each season's colors accordingly.

She said, "I'll make arrangements to have the wine shipped to Berkeley."

"That's fine by me. Alix tends to worry."

"I'll leave a few bottles for you. I'd like to start sharing it with friends. And tell Alix I'm not going to abuse it, just enjoy it."

The snow fell through midday but by evening the streets were clear, the house filling up with guests.

"A small party," Sophie said, "just a few friends."

Sandra watched the crowd gather, thinking of

Amy, thinking of Jay. Conversations swirled around her, melting like snowflakes when she tried to catch their meaning. She moved to stand again at the window, dark streets disappearing beyond the room's bright reflection, one more storm completed.

# Chapter 19

Sandra flew into Oakland in the early morning darkness on the last day of the year. She took a train and a taxi home and left her bag unpacked in the hall. She put her feet up on the couch and fell asleep, waking several hours later, surprisingly refreshed. Sunlight shone with determination although the temperature, by West Coast standards, remained cold.

Ignoring her suitcase, Sandra picked up the phone, but Jay didn't answer at home and a machine clicked on at her shop.

"Jay, it's Sandra. My flight got in this morning —"

"Welcome home." Jay's voice cut in on the line.

"Are you very busy?"

"I'm closed for inventory. How was your trip?"

"It's good to be back."

"Does that mean you're getting used to our weather?"

Sandra said, "I believe I'm starting to develop a preference for beaches."

"Can I see you? I can be there in fifteen minutes."

"Hurry."

The Dodge was at her house in ten minutes. Jay drove them to Point Reyes, a long peninsula of land boasting an abundance of wildlife. Warmly layered against the wind, groups of hearty whale-watchers staked out vantage points. Jay parked in a sheltered cove away from the binocular-clad crowd.

They walked along the beach, Sandra exclaiming over pools revealed at low tide. An underwater rainbow of starfish sparkled in shallow water.

"I had no idea they were so lovely," she murmured.

Jay led them out of the wind into the protection of low dunes, shaking out a blanket and producing a thermos from her knapsack. Sandra savored the flavor of strong coffee.

"I should have known." She smiled. "It's good to see you, Jay."

Jackets and sweaters became a nest and gentle passion a furnace. They made love softly, undisturbed by wind and waves, movement as delicate as shells in shallow pools, and emotion like light on water.

\* \* \* \* \*

Jay pulled a sweater over her head. "Do you have plans for tonight?"

Sandra stroked her fingers through Jay's hair, setting loose an accidental spray of sand. Jay blinked in surprise as Sandra gently brushed away the grains.

"I don't have any plans."

Jay wrapped a jacket around Sandra's shoulders. "Jonathan's party is tonight. Would you like to go?"

"I'd love to."

Jay stood, helping her to her feet.

"I'll have to go home for a change of clothes," Sandra remarked, brushing sand from her jeans.

"We have plenty of time." Jay paused. "Would you like to see my place?"

Sandra smiled and said again, "I'd love to."

Jay turned away, gathering up the blanket and the rest of their belongings, but not before Sandra saw uncertainty in Jay's eyes. Something else was there as well. What on earth, Sandra wondered, was Jay afraid of?

They drove back to Berkeley as slanting rays of sun pierced the car. Sandra watched Jay's profile in the late afternoon warmth.

Jay kept her eyes on the road. "What's on your mind, love?"

"I was thinking about the sun on the hills behind my house," Sandra answered. "It was the first thing I loved about Berkeley."

Jay laughed. "Are you hungry?"

Sandra grinned at the familiar question. "Yes, quite."

"How about Chinese?"

"Sounds great." Sandra reached to stroke sun-stained hair. "I wondered when you'd get around to showing me where you live."

"I meant to show you a thousand times."

"Why didn't you?"

"Because you like me, you like the store, you're interested in my school work. I guess I'm trying to show you what I think you want to see."

"I like who you are, Jay. Is what you do so important?"

"Isn't it? Whether or not I have a degree, if I sell things and make money, it matters to people."

"What matters to you?"

"I'll show you." Jay turned the wheel of the car. "There's a take-out place around the corner."

Jay lived on the top floor of an old house. They entered the kitchen from an outside flight of stairs. Sandra helped Jay unload cartons of food onto a redwood table and then left the kitchen to explore.

Walls had been removed at the front of the house and Sandra walked through the open expanse in amazement. The floor was bare hardwood. A west-facing window showcased the bay, and a long futon folded into a frame beneath the view. A workbench lined the opposing wall under skylights that Sandra guessed would bring in morning sun.

Everywhere else Sandra looked she saw wood. Pieces of every size, color and texture were stacked neatly in bins; smaller strips lay scattered under shelves holding tools that Sandra couldn't begin to name. Bookshelves contained small finished pieces, and she ran her fingers over polished grain. Utilitarian and abstract, boxes and cups mingled with wood that was carved simply to please the eye and engage the touch.

As she turned from the shelves to the center of the room, an almost tangible force rose to meet her. Large, free-standing sculptures seemed to grow from the bare floor. The wood looked still alive, layers peeled back to reveal the beauty beneath the bark. A bench could have been a trunk leaning against the wind. Rounded wardrobes arched, willow-like. Wood glowed as if sunlight still warmed the leaves.

Sandra glanced up. Jay had emerged from the kitchen to stand patiently during the silent inspection.

"You're an artist." Sandra spoke the simple fact with faint surprise. Muted by the power of the wood, her words sounded hushed in her own ears. "Magnificent. I should have guessed . . ."

"Why are you surprised?"

"Why do you hide it?" Her voice cracked. She felt the strength of wood at her back pulsing through the room. Anger crested within her leaving a swell of grief. She repeated, "How can you hide it?"

"Practice," Jay said calmly. "Come on, let's eat."

Sandra stood quietly in the kitchen. After several moments she said, "It feels like returning to the modern world after visiting a primeval forest."

Jay spooned rice and vegetables into ceramic bowls. She raised an eyebrow, mocking Sandra's seriousness.

"Damnit, Jay, your work is magnificent. Why haven't you said anything about it?"

"I sell a few pieces here and there, mostly through Kozy, or Jonathan's connections."

"That's not what I asked."

Jay pushed a bowl across the table. "If you had the opportunity to show your most private self in public, would you bare your soul to the world?"

Stunned, Sandra said, "You had me fooled. I thought your passion was in your antiques. But that's just a compromise for you."

"A ruse, really."

"Are you that scared of your family?"

"Failure scares me. My family thinks I've failed at academics. How can I fail at something I care nothing about? I care about my art, so I protect it."

"You hide it." Tension whipped through Sandra's words. "You have your excuses all lined up — the business, the family fortune. What about me, Jay? Am I just an academic distraction?"

"You underestimate yourself," Jay said quietly. "Falling in love with you has been an inspiration."

Sandra felt the presence of the sculpture again at her back, the kitchen no longer a haven from the raw strength of art. She stared at the bowls of untouched food. She could smell the scent of wood. She waited silently, testing her own separate stand of courage.

"Your honesty has always been unyielding," she said at last. "I love you, too."

Jay stepped around the table, pulling Sandra into her arms. She whispered, "Let's get you some clothes that aren't full of sand."

"We should eat," Sandra protested.

Jay brushed her lips against Sandra's hair. "There's going to be plenty of food at the party. Most of it better than soggy Chinese."

"If I get out of these clothes one more time," Sandra threatened, "I'm not going to put them back on."

Jay smiled, moving her hands to find the space between clothing and skin. "Tell me what you need. I'll drive to your place while you shower."

Sandra let Jay lift her sweater over her head. Then wool fell to wood in a sprinkling of sand.

# Chapter 20

"I've been looking forward to meeting your friends." Sandra walked with Jay up the drive to Jonathan's spacious home.

"They're good people," Jay said seriously. She took Sandra's hand. "I'm glad you're here."

Jonathan met them at the door. "Ladies, come in, come in. Don't be shy." He took Sandra's hand in both of his own. "Happy New Year, Sandra. I'm delighted to have you here."

Sandra returned his warm greeting. "Thank you, Jonathan. The pleasure is mine."

Jonathan released Sandra and kissed Jay on the cheek, holding Jay as she hugged him tightly.

"I love you, Jon."

When Jay let go, Jonathan smiled through his tears. He said, "Love is almost enough, isn't it?"

Sandra hesitated, reluctant to interrupt the private moment. She turned as another guest appeared in the entryway.

Kozy stepped forward. "Dry your tears, Jon," she scolded gently. "You have a house full of guests to look after."

Jonathan produced a silk handkerchief and blew his nose energetically.

"Crying in dress clothes is such a hassle." He sighed. "My apologies. Please," he gestured to Sandra, "come join us."

Kozy took Jonathan's arm, steering the group into the party. The house had been festively prepared, but Sandra suspected that no amount of decoration could cover Michael's absence. Lights seemed a little too bright, guests a little too subdued. Jazz music only sounded melancholy. Sandra moved to stand by the fire, which tried to lend warmth, if not good cheer. Jay and Kozy joined her.

Jay asked, "Is this a gallant effort or a depressing attempt?"

"Both," Kozy replied.

Sandra considered the choices of grief — to cover the space or give in to emptiness. Friendship fought the loneliness; sometimes it helped.

Kozy said, "How about some brandy?"

"On my way." Jay headed for the bar.

She returned with Jonathan, who balanced a tray of glasses and passed out snifters with practiced ease.

"Now," Kozy raised her glass for a toast. "Lighten up. For heaven's sake, we had the wake already. This is supposed to be a party."

Jay's surprised laughter broke the shocked silence. Sandra watched the lines of fatigue around Jonathan's mouth. After a moment, they eased slightly and he also began to laugh.

Heads turned as Jay and Jonathan laughed in earnest. The feeling of hushed tension diminished. Voices increased in volume and glasses clinked merrily.

Jonathan turned to Kozy. "I'm so glad you came to my party. Please excuse me," he added with a small bow to the group. "I believe I have some entertaining to do."

Jay raised her glass to Kozy. "You're a good friend."

Sandra stood beside Jay. She placed a hand at the back of Jay's neck, grazing her fingers through the soft hair at Jay's collar. Jay's arm circled Sandra's waist, holding her close. A late guest entered the room.

Sandra's fingers froze on the back of Jay's neck as Audrey Linden stood inside the doorway. Sandra let her hand fall stiffly to her side.

"I didn't think Jon knew Audrey," Jay commented.

Kozy said, "I invited her."

Jay choked on a swallow of brandy. "Did I just call you a good friend?"

Kozy nodded. "You did."

Sandra watched as Audrey made her own introductions and accepted a glass of champagne, then walked with assurance across the room.

Kozy stepped forward to greet her, and Audrey pressed her mouth briefly but tenderly to Kozy's lips.

"Well, well," Jay murmured.

Audrey inclined her head while Kozy whispered something, then she met Jay's stare.

"Hello, Jay." Audrey turned to Sandra. "Sandra, good evening."

Sandra took a breath. "Hello, Audrey. You're becoming quite an ally."

Audrey nodded. "How was Boston?"

"I'm glad to be back."

Sandra felt Jay's arm tighten around her and she glanced apprehensively at Jay. Jay was gripping her glass so hard that Sandra feared it might shatter in her hand. She reached to take the snifter. Jay resisted for a moment, then let go. Amber liquid splashed above the rim. Sandra set her own glass and Jay's aside, dabbing at her hand with a paper napkin.

Jay looked at Kozy. "How long?"

"Several months, Jay."

"Oh."

Jay considered Audrey somberly. "It's hard to keep enemies when they start sleeping with your friends."

Audrey said, "I'm not your enemy, Jay."

"Kozy, I'm curious," Jay asked. "Why didn't you tell me?"

"I asked her not to," Audrey interjected.

Sandra crumpled the napkin she was holding into a ball. She turned impatiently toward the fire and moved the wire screen, tossing the paper onto the flames. She replaced the screen and returned to Jay's side.

Audrey met Sandra's gaze. "You think I'm a hypocrite, Sandra?"

"Your words," Sandra replied.

Kozy started to speak but Audrey touched her arm. "Don't defend me, dear. Sandra has every reason to consider my silence a betrayal."

Sandra shook her head. "Your silence hurts Jay, not me. She's the one you tried to influence. You have no right to hide from her."

Jay said sarcastically, "Is a coming out party in order?"

Sandra winced at Jay's tone but Audrey said calmly, "Nonsense. Lesbianism isn't new to me. Openness is new." Audrey looked at Sandra. "I thought by rejecting fear, I had defeated it. I was wrong. I'm sorry."

Sandra said quietly, "Exposure isn't easy for anyone."

"Oh, this is just great," Jay snarled. "We're all getting so close." Jay looked around the room. "I wonder what the boys are up to?"

Sandra linked her fingers through Jay's and hung on.

Kozy said firmly, "Jay, your fight with Audrey isn't about her choice of lovers."

"You think you know what this is about?" Jay's voice strained in a low whisper. "Enlighten me."

"Your silence is as hurtful as anyone's," Kozy said. "You're smothering yourself, Jay. When are you going to stop hiding from your talent?"

"You have no right . . ." Jay snapped off the ends of her words.

"What about me, Jay?" Sandra said gently, "Do I have the right to ask?"

Audrey spoke before Jay could reply. "If you and Sandra don't mind leaving the party early, there's something I'd like to show you."

Jay crossed her arms. "This is Jon's party. He needs us here."

Kozy gestured to the buffet table where Jonathan and several young men were replenishing hors d'oeuvres.

"Hey, Jon, put on some real music. Let's dance," someone complained.

Jonathan put his hands on hips. "Can't you appreciate the classics?"

He dropped the pose as he caught Kozy's eye. A blare of music followed him across the room. He bent his head to hear Kozy and then kissed her lightly.

"Drive safely." He turned to Jay. "Happy New Year, Jay."

"What the hell do you know about this?" Jay demanded.

Jonathan stepped closer to Jay. Sandra could barely hear his soft words. "You can't wait forever," he whispered.

He glanced sympathetically at Sandra and rejoined his party.

Jay's eyes searched the room and found the glass of brandy Sandra had set aside. She reached it in a stride and drained it in a swallow. She pulled car keys from her pocket and handed them to Sandra.

"Drive safely," she muttered.

Sandra accepted the keys and took Jay's arm, following Kozy and Audrey outside. The cool, dry air held no trace of fog. Sandra shivered.

Audrey opened the passenger door on an ancient Mercedes and helped Kozy inside.

Jay paused at the curb. "Want to tell me where we're going?"

"My house." Audrey instructed, "Follow us."

"Follow Audrey," Jay directed.

Sandra got in behind the wheel. "I'm not going to let them out of my sight."

Sandra followed the old Mercedes across the bridge to San Francisco. Audrey snugged her wheels expertly against a steep curb and Sandra struggled to do the same with Jay's Dodge. They were in an old Victorian neighborhood.

"Audrey's house seems well-suited to her," Sandra commented.

Jay asked, "Weren't the Victorians known for hiding great passions?"

Sandra stepped out of the car. Tall houses rose elegantly, bright colors muted in moonlight. The color saved the architecture from arrogance, as though strict occupants had let laughter escape, washing the neighborhood in an afterthought of good humor.

Audrey led the way up narrow steps. She pushed the door open and said, "Please come in."

Inside, silver shadows filtered through a bay window. Sandra had the impression of wood, moonlight in a forest.

Audrey switched on a lamp, bringing the room to light in a soft glow. Sandra heard Jay's gasp. She turned to see Jay staring first at the room, then at Audrey.

"At first it was hard to get," Audrey told Jay. "You sell so sparingly. I began to collect seriously when I met Kozy."

Jay glanced at Kozy. "You seduced her with my furniture?"

Kozy smiled. "In a word, yes." She crossed her arms against Jay's glare. "Let's get clear on one point, Jay. Audrey's not in love with you, just your wood. Honestly, look around."

Sandra turned to face the full impact of Jay's creativity. Starkly graceful, subtly fertile, the room came alive with the form and force of nature. There were probably a dozen pieces.

Jay said softly, "I try to anticipate my customers. But I never let myself imagine..." Her voice faltered. "Audrey, why did you bring me here?"

"Everyone has a right to know of their impact on others. I've loved your work for years. I wanted to share that with you."

When no one spoke for several moments, Kozy suggested, "How about coffee?"

Audrey indicated the sofa. "Please, sit down."

When Jay and Sandra were seated, Audrey chose a wooden chair for herself. Sandra studied the chair's design. Its back and arms flared softly, sculpted so thinly as to be almost transparent. A delicate throne.

"One of the first pieces I bought," Audrey said, following Sandra's gaze.

An awkward silence carried the clatter of dishes.

"Has she taken over your kitchen?" Jay asked.

Audrey nodded. "I'm afraid so."

Kozy returned carrying a tray of mugs and a pot of coffee. She set out cream and sugar and poured graciously. The simple ritual eased but couldn't erase the tension.

Kozy seated herself in a matching chair next to Audrey's. "I spoke with Jonathan yesterday," she said mildly. "Jack called again."

"The doctor's cousin," Jay explained to Sandra's questioning look. "The artist in New York."

"He's impatient. He needs a partner and he's not going to wait much longer. You'll have to make a decision, Jay." Kozy paused. "Jon and I would like to renew our offer."

Jay propped her elbows on her knees and rubbed her face with her hands. Sandra felt the remaining tension drain away. When Jay looked up, Sandra could see the fatigue etched on her face. She looked exhausted. "Are you planning an auction?" she asked.

"Jon's ready to set a date."

Jay pushed herself up from the sofa. "I'll give you an answer tomorrow." She held out a hand to Sandra and said, "Let's go."

Sandra walked to the door without a word. Jay pulled it open, then stopped.

"Kozy," Jay called. "If there's an auction, bring your girlfriend. It's going to cost her."

Sandra gripped Jay's keys and walked outside.

Jay sagged against the car. "Can you get us to my place?"

Sandra nodded.

Jay jumped at a sudden, sharp explosion of noise. Startled, Sandra looked up. The moon was gone, replaced by the falling colors of fireworks.

"Damn," Jay muttered. "I forgot." She looked at Sandra. "Happy New Year."

Sandra kissed Jay. "Happy New Year."

# Chapter 21

Jay kicked off her boots and slumped onto the futon in her studio. Sandra sat down beside her, reaching for Jay's hand. She stroked the long fingers, then brought Jay's hand to her lips. She kissed the fingers, the palm. Then she clasped Jay's hand with her own and sighed.

"This isn't new."

Jay gave Sandra's hand a squeeze. "Kozy and Jon offered to buy the antiques business. It will be good for Jon, now that Michael's gone."

"What's good for you, Jay?"

Jay gave a tired smile. "You're good for me. I love you."

Sandra thought of Jonathan's sad words. "Is it enough?"

Jay snapped, "Why should I lose this relationship? So that Audrey can sit in pretty chairs?"

"I'll fight Audrey every step of the way," Sandra said, "if that's what you want." She studied Jay's eyes. "Tell me the truth."

"I want you," Jay repeated.

The words were on the edge of Sandra's tongue — the question she no longer feared, the answer she had learned to speak.

"Jay," she whispered, "there's no safe haven. Can you accept the risk of your own passion?"

Jay closed her eyes. She brought Sandra's hand to her mouth, then pressed it against her cheek. She opened her eyes and asked, "Did you find what you were looking for in Boston?"

Sandra smiled. "I found good friends and old memories. And I realized that I want to live my life here."

"Will you live here without me?"

"Yes."

Jay stood up. "Come with me. I want to show you more."

Sandra followed Jay down a short hallway, past the bedroom to the back of the house.

"This used to be a porch," Jay said. "I had it converted when I took the walls down in the front room."

A low window looked down on the bay. Sandra glimpsed an edge of the campus, indistinct in the darkness. The room was uncluttered, almost empty except for a stack of drawings on a drafting table. A single shelf above the table held three small sculptures. Jay took them down and set them on the window sill. Each carving showed a woman, stylized, the wood merely hinting at hips and breasts. They seemed to be part of a series.

Sandra lifted the first figure and stroked the smooth form with her hand. Red-hued wood was warm to her touch. The sculpted woman stood before a wall, the wood mirroring her image. The brass plaque at the base read *Woman and Reflection*. In the second sculpture, the woman stood before a large wave that curled above her, ready to engulf her. *Woman at Water's Edge*.

Sandra lifted the final piece. The last figure showed the same woman but she was changing back into the wood, her raised arms like branches, her legs molded into the trunk of a tree. Sandra caressed the soft wood. The base said, *Transformation*.

Sandra returned the final carving to the sill. She wrapped her arms around herself and stared at the window but the distance blurred with her tears.

"I tried, but I couldn't get it right." Jay's voice was husky.

*If I could only paint the light on the water, I would be happy*. Sandra heard the old words echo. Her tears falling freely, she turned toward Jay.

"I'm so sorry," Jay whispered. "I need to learn more . . . I want so much to put the feelings in the wood."

"I think," Sandra said steadily, "I think you got it just right."

Jay moved to embrace her as Sandra cried, and Sandra felt on her own face the wetness of Jay's tears. They stood together like that for a very long time.


A distant clatter tapped insistently through layers of sleep. Sandra awakened slowly, turning, reaching for Jay only to find an empty bed. She came fully awake and sat up.

Jay's bedroom, like the drafting room she had seen the night before, was small and free of clutter. A pair of framed watercolors bearing Evie Kaplan's signature decorated the walls, otherwise, the space contained few personal items.

Jay lived, obviously, in the open front studio that held her imprint and showcased her spirit. One could never know Jay, Sandra reflected, unless they had stood with her art, surrounded by wood. She wondered if Roberta Hope had ever visited her daughter at home.

"Hi. Want some coffee?" Jay spoke from the bedroom door, a steaming mug in her hands.

"Yes. Why don't you bring that over here."

Jay pushed a pillow against the bedframe and swung her legs up beside Sandra. She wore faded jeans and a T-shirt. Sandra accepted the coffee, aware of her own nakedness. She watched Jay's eyes follow the sway of her breasts as she lifted the cup to drink. Copper eyes warmed her more than the liquid.

"Breakfast is almost ready," Jay murmured.

Steam from the coffee curled around Jay's fingers

as she reached to take the mug from Sandra's hand. She turned slightly to set the cup aside and Sandra followed with her body. She slipped the T-shirt up and over Jay's head as she lowered her lips to Jay's shoulder. Jay rolled onto her back, inhaling deeply, and Sandra took the raised breast into her mouth. She felt Jay's hands on her own breasts, molding and shaping the softness between them, finding the form of love.

Sandra moved her mouth lower, letting her tongue taste the ridges of rib and muscle along Jay's flank. She slipped a hand into the waist of Jay's jeans, then used both hands to free the fastenings. Jay lifted her hips and Sandra pulled fabric away. Sandra slipped herself over a thigh, taking Jay's breast again into her mouth.

Jay touched Sandra's face, and soft words whispered a request at Sandra's ear. Sandra brushed her answer against Jay's lips. Holding Jay's face in her hands, Sandra kissed her deeply. Jay moved away, and she repeated the soft words.

Sandra said, "Yes, I want that, too."

She shifted her weight, turning while Jay pulled the covers around them both. She felt Jay's hands steadying her hips while she raised herself over the lushness of Jay.

She heard Jay whisper, "Is it okay?"

In answer, Sandra pushed Jay's thighs gently apart. She stroked the tender skin until it parted, fragrant and glistening beneath her touch. Then Sandra lowered herself onto Jay, opening herself to Jay, bending to take Jay fully into her mouth.

Tears formed at the edge of her eyes and she blinked, pressing herself to the center of Jay, settling toward her own center. Then the tears escaped, mixing with Jay's spreading wetness, and she closed her eyes, immersing herself in an ocean of moisture and emotion.

The tide of her pulse ebbed and flowed, steady and soothing, a current of comfort washing through her, no longer surging, softening to an absolute stillness.

Sandra listened to her own breathing. She lay, gently flushed, in a tangle of arms and legs. She tried to sit up but an arm caught and held her. She located a dark head in the chaos of sheets and ran her fingers through Jay's hair. Wet copper eyes met her gaze.

Jay said, "I'll visit now and then if you don't mind."

"I'll miss you." Sandra stroked, then tousled Jay's head. "I need a shower," she said in an almost normal tone of voice. "And you, darling, unless I miss my guess, must be starving."

Sandra watched as Jay folded eggs over cheese into the uneven shape of an omelette.

"I didn't know you cooked."

"With my appetite?" Jay smiled. "I had to learn." Jay set plates of food on the table and sat down. "I'm scared for you, Sandra. I never meant for you to make enemies."

Sandra took a bite, then said, "We've both taken an unpopular stand. The world is full of critics eager to sit in judgment."

Jay chased a bit of egg around her plate. "I don't relish criticism. Why does it seem unavoidable?"

Sandra sipped her coffee. "Jay, when you sat in my office and told me you wanted to run like hell —"

"Did I know I was going to sail past acceptance only to embrace my own ambition?" Jay interrupted with a shake of her head. "Did you understand that teaching me might cost you a career?"

Sandra helped herself to more eggs. "Run your own race, Jay. I'll certainly fight my own battles."

Jay reached for the coffee pot as a knock sounded at the kitchen door.

"Expecting company?"

"No." Jay crossed the kitchen and pulled open the door.

"Good morning, Jessica." Roberta Hope held a statuesque pose on the doorstep.

Jay said bluntly, "I didn't think you knew where I lived."

"Of course I know where you live, Jessica, and I believe this visit is long overdue. May I come in?"

Jay moved aside, allowing her mother to enter. Roberta took one step and froze when she saw Sandra. Sandra silently thanked all of the gods in which she didn't believe that she had changed out of Jay's bathrobe into her own jeans and sweater.

She raised her mug in greeting. "Good morning, Roberta."

"Dr. Ross."

"Please, call me Sandra. Would you care for coffee?"

"Thank you." Roberta continued to stand, unmoving. Jay glanced warily from her mother to Sandra.

"Jay, darling," Sandra said calmly, "pour your mother a cup of coffee."

Roberta said grimly, "It's true, then."

Sandra replied, "Yes."

"Then there's no reason for me to stay."

Roberta turned toward the door but Jay was a step ahead of her. "Sit down, Mother."

"I'm sorry, Jessica. I was obviously in error to come here and I will leave now."

Jay leaned against the closed door and crossed her arms. "I'd like to hear what you came to say."

"As would I," Sandra concurred.

Roberta took a moment to collect herself. She turned back to Sandra, a smile tightly in place. "Very well." She seated herself. "I'll have coffee now if you don't mind, Jessica."

Jay set another mug of coffee on the table. Sandra placed cream and sugar within Roberta's reach. Jay remained standing, leaning against the counter behind Sandra.

"Sam is worried that you won't stay in school," Roberta stated.

"I've decided to move to New York."

"And throw away your future, just like that?" Roberta flashed a look at Sandra but she continued to address Jay. She said bitterly, "Is she worth it?"

Sandra swallowed coffee, waiting for Jay to respond.

"You know, Mother, you and I aren't really so different."

Sandra turned slightly, trying to watch Jay's expression.

"We both know how to appreciate investment and return." Jay gestured to Sandra. "What's a fair price for love?" Anger edged her voice as she urged, "Go ahead, Mom, make your best bid on my life."

"Just tell me why." Roberta raised her hands, palms up. "You don't like school, you don't care about your trust fund. All right. Fine." She slapped the table. "Tell me why." She pleaded, "What do you want, Jessica?"

Jay said slowly, "This is quite possibly the first time you've ever stopped to ask me what I want."

"I'm asking now."

Jay sighed. "This seems to be my week to go public. Okay, I'll show you."

Jay left the kitchen. Roberta glanced at Sandra, then followed Jay. Sandra waited a heartbeat, then followed. She watched as Roberta walked the expanse of studio floor. She saw Roberta stroke a palm along the wood; Sandra remembered the feel of the grain. Rather than savor the texture, Roberta crossed her arms.

"Impressive." The word pressed grudgingly through Roberta's lips. "And this is more meaningful to you than an education?"

Jay tucked her hands into the back pockets of her jeans. "Yes."

"I'm sorry, Jessica. I just can't accept . . . this." Roberta swept an arm, including Sandra as well as the furniture in her gesture.

"Funny thing." Jay shrugged. "Your acceptance matters less to me than I thought." She paused. "Tell you what, Mom. I'll send you my address when I'm in New York. If you decide you want to get to know me, come for a visit. Otherwise, I'll probably remember to send a Christmas card next year."

Roberta's hard eyes hunted for Sandra. "I hold you responsible," she hissed.

Jay took a step but Sandra motioned her back. "Roberta." Sandra kept her voice firm and pleasant. "I have always been impressed by the level of fundraising you achieve at the foundation." Sandra crossed the studio and placed her hand on a bookshelf full of wood. "Jay's sculpture will certainly be popular among your benefactors. However —" Sandra looked directly at Roberta — "some donors may be distressed to learn that you tried to barter your daughter's trust fund for academic influence." Sandra smiled at Jay. "I'm sure Jay will keep her customers informed."

Roberta gave Sandra an icy stare, but Jay spoke first.

"Lose the attitude, Mom. If I were you, I'd consider your options. You might have better luck against the NRA."

Sandra went back to the kitchen. She called over her shoulder, "I'll make a fresh pot of coffee."

Several long moments later, Jay and Roberta joined her in the kitchen.

Roberta said, "Thank you, but I must decline the coffee. Good-bye, Jessica." She added abruptly, "Perhaps we can arrange a visit."

Sandra waited until the door closed and then set the coffee pot on the counter with a shaky hand.

"Do me a favor." Sandra smiled. "Invite me to New York when your mother's not around."

Jay moved to Sandra, gathering her into an embrace.

"Oh, and another thing."

Jay looked at Sandra, a question in her eyes.

"Be sure to invite me to the auction. I'm going to give Audrey a run for her money."

Jay laughed and kissed her. She whispered, "Audrey can't have everything."

# Chapter 22

The new semester began with a flurry of paperwork. Sandra pushed open the door to her office and dropped an armload of books onto her desk with an indelicate grunt. Whatever had possessed her to enter the building through the far wing? She'd wasted ten minutes trying to find her office in the unfamiliar maze. She smiled. Her arms were tired but she had enjoyed the detour.

A brief knock sounded at the door and Sam Kaplan's head appeared around the frame. "How are your new classes?"

"Too big. I'll have to assign extra reading and see who drops."

"A good strategy." The elderly man cleared his throat. "Did you know that Jessica Hope submitted her research paper during the holiday break?"

"Yes."

Sam shifted his weight from one foot to the other. "The news won't be official for another week, but the committee plans to accept the paper and recommend her for advanced standing."

"Jay left yesterday for New York, but I'm not surprised. It was an excellent paper." She added softly to herself, "And not all answers are academic."

Sam commented, "You seem to have weathered the storm."

"I was under the impression that no one remained unscathed."

"Roberta Hope has hired an attorney," he said. "It looks like she's planning to fight the National Rifle Association over the terms of the trust." He hesitated. "Amy Greenburg told me you'll be riding off into the sunset."

"Amy knows that I'm staying right here. In fact, she's planning to take me sightseeing in San Francisco."

"Good luck with your classes." The department chair strode away, already intent on other concerns.

Sandra walked to the window to consider California's invisible progress through winter. The empty bench continued to wait for inspiration. Her own transformation seemed equally invisible but creativity had not, after all, been abandoned. Line after line, her work grew with substance, and she had no doubt that the words would carry her through spring.

The sun broke out of low clouds and green leaves turned copper in the light. Sandra pushed open the window and reached to touch rough bark. She stayed for a moment leaning into the air, balanced between hills and bay, certain of an edge on which she had found plenty of room to stand.

**A few of the publications of**
**THE NAIAD PRESS, INC.**
**P.O. Box 10543 • Tallahassee, Florida 32302**
**Phone (904) 539-5965**
**Toll-Free Order Number: 1-800-533-1973**
*Mail orders welcome. Please include 15% postage.*

THE COLOR OF WINTER by Lisa Shapiro. 208 pp. Romantic love beyond your wildest dreams. ISBN 1-56280-116-3   $10.95

FAMILY SECRETS by Laura DeHart Young. 208 pp. Enthralling romance and suspense. ISBN 1-56280-119-8   10.95

INLAND PASSAGE by Jane Rule. 288 pp. Tales exploring conventional & unconventional relationships. ISBN 0-930044-56-8   10.95

DOUBLE BLUFF by Claire McNab. 208 pp. 7th Detective Carol Ashton Mystery. ISBN 1-56280-096-5   10.95

BAR GIRLS by Lauran Hoffman. 176 pp. See the movie, read the book! ISBN 1-56280-115-5   10.95

THE FIRST TIME EVER edited by Barbara Grier & Christine Cassidy. 272 pp. Love stories by Naiad Press authors. ISBN 1-56280-086-8   14.95

MISS PETTIBONE AND MISS McGRAW by Brenda Weathers. 208 pp. A charming ghostly love story. ISBN 1-56280-151-1   10.95

CHANGES by Jackie Calhoun. 208 pp. Involved romance and relationships. ISBN 1-56280-083-3   10.95

FAIR PLAY by Rose Beecham. 256 pp. 3rd Amanda Valentine Mystery. ISBN 1-56280-081-7   10.95

PAXTON COURT by Diane Salvatore. 256 pp. Erotic and wickedly funny contemporary tale about the business of learning to live together. ISBN 1-56280-109-0   21.95

PAYBACK by Celia Cohen. 176 pp. A gripping thriller of romance, revenge and betrayal. ISBN 1-56280-084-1   10.95

THE BEACH AFFAIR by Barbara Johnson. 224 pp. Sizzling summer romance/mystery/intrigue. ISBN 1-56280-090-6   10.95

These are just a few of the many Naiad Press titles — we are the oldest and largest lesbian/feminist publishing company in the world. Please request a complete catalog. We offer personal service; we encourage and welcome direct mail orders from individuals who have limited access to bookstores carrying our publications.